A Taste of Christmas

Rachel Bowdler

Content Warnings

Gambling addiction

Poverty and homelessness

Strong language

Minor injury

Mentions of death, loss, and childhood neglect

Toxic past relationship

For Yorkshire puddings:
this is my love letter to you.

One

Erin Levine marched into the hectic kitchen of Spuds 'n' Puds and halted with a vehement sniff, the heels of her pumps clicking against the freshly mopped tiles. Was she not distracted by the ominous, overly-familiar smell of something charred, she might have rolled her eyes at the way her catering staff seemed to shrink just slightly. Cowards, the lot of them. They'd be no good on *Hell's Kitchen* with Gordon Ramsay cursing them out over their shoulder.

She channelled that sort of blazing aggression now just to prove it. "Mavis, you better not be burning the fucking potatoes again!"

"Nope." Mavis' frail voice drifted from somewhere behind the scorching stoves. She appeared a moment later with two plates of jacket potatoes in her hands, ready for service. They held no sign of burns yet, thank goodness. "The potatoes are right as rain today. Promise."

"Then what's burning?"

A shrug from Mavis. The other staff members avoided eye contact with Erin as she made her way around the kitchen slowly.

"Oh, stop crying, Derek," she muttered when

1

she came across her particularly sweaty sous-chef, who had only been promoted because her usual was on maternity leave. "Take five and pull yourself together."

"It's that line chef of yours, miss," he blubbered. "Threatened to throw me gravy over me head when it started sticking t'pan."

Erin raised an eyebrow and crossed her arms, her steely gaze searching for her line chef — and boyfriend — in a sea of colliding white-uniformed bodies. She caught him by the back stoves, sprinkling something into a pot.

Was that bloody *parsley*?

"*Luca!*" A fresh wave of anger roiled through Erin as she made her way to stop the demise of her beloved gravy recipe. Her beloved gravy recipe that definitely did *not* include parsley as an ingredient — nor, as a fifty-year-old recipe inherited from Erin's mother, who had gotten it from *her* father, had it ever. "What on earth are you doing to my gravy?"

Luca's chiselled features melted into those of a criminal who had just been caught red-handed. He hopped away from the stove and attempted to hide his contraband behind his back. "Nothing, nothing, nothing."

With a sigh, Erin wriggled around his narrow frame to snatch the fresh herbs. "If you can't follow my recipes, I'll hire someone who can."

"*Oof.*" His lips curled with a cheeky grin, eyes twinkling with a mischief that Erin always

2

had to look away from unless they were in the bedroom. "You're sexy when you're angry with me, Miss Levine."

She shushed him, glancing around to make sure nobody else had heard. If someone found out she had let her line chef into her bed, all semblance of the authority she held in here would crumble in an instant. It had never been supposed to happen at all... but she was only a woman after all. When an attractive Italian man with curly hair and a smouldering accent walked into her restaurant and impressed her with his cooking talents, well... she was only human. Pretty Italians who also happened to be quite good in bed weren't easy to come by in the middle of Manchester, and Erin was nothing if not an opportunist.

But if Luca D'Angelo kept scaring away her staff and changing up Erin's very clear rules and recipes, Erin would have no choice but to sack him off professionally or otherwise, charm and talent be damned. A slick, oily feeling had begun to fester in her gut whenever they were in the kitchen together; with it, the sense that Luca thought he knew better than her and wasn't afraid to undermine her to show it. She could understand why, she supposed. A man with a decade's worth of international experience cooking in all sorts of restaurants, working in a typically British restaurant best known for its Yorkshire pudding wraps and jacket potatoes...

His being here didn't really make sense at

all. But this was Erin's empire, and she was the executive chef, and she loved this place too much to let anyone take over. She doubted that if she was a man, she'd have the same concerns.

"I was told you threatened Derek," she accused, narrowing her eyes to show Luca that this was no longer a little game to be continued later on, when the restaurant closed and they were alone.

"'Threatened' is a strong word." Luca shrugged dismissively, dropping the parsley and stirring the pot of gravy. Erin snatched the herbs from the chopping board and threw them straight in the bin.

"You made him cry."

"He is a sensitive soul."

Erin huffed impatiently. "I'm sure I don't need to remind you who's in charge in this kitchen, Mr. D'Angelo. Don't be a dick to your co-workers — especially not your superiors."

"Pfft. I should be sous-chef and you know it. Derek is useless."

She gritted her teeth. The problem was that over the four-year course of her management here, she'd tried to be the kind, understanding boss, *and* the chummy one who the waiters always invited for drinks after their shifts, *and* the passive one who left the kitchen staff alone to get on with it themselves. None of them had worked, and she'd grown tired of expecting everybody to treat her like the leader she was, tired of being talked about for not being good at her job or for trying too hard. She was a leader, and now people knew it. The best thing she could do was assert her dominance; make sure that everybody knew she expected the best and wasn't afraid to say so. This was a business — *her* business — and she'd fight tooth and claw to keep it not just running, but successful. Even if it meant being stern and disliked. Even if it meant ending personal relationships in the process.

"You're needed outside for a moment, Erin." It was Frankie, one of the new seasonal hires, lingering at Erin's shoulder. With the Christmas markets stationed on the cobbled, busy street outside the restaurant and their takeaway window open for passersby, Erin had been in dire need of new staff.

She nodded tersely and followed Frankie through the already packed restaurant, casting amicable smiles to the patrons. "What's it like out there?"

"Jam-packed." Frankie blew out a breath, disrupting her sweat-dampened fringe. She was rosy-cheeked and wide-eyed, and Erin wondered if she'd be getting another resignation before the week was up. The catering industry was certainly not for the faint of heart, and more staff came and went through these doors than customers at this time of year.

"Good." They stepped out through the tinsel-strewn glass door, the icy December air a welcome reprieve from the kitchen's heat. Beneath golden, globular fairy lights, a long line of customers queued for their Yorkshire pudding-wrapped roast dinners at the takeaway window, their gloved hands wrapped around mugs of *Glühwein* and their breath fogging the air. To say it was only the first day of this year's markets, the rest of the stalls seemed swamped, too. George's cheese samples were being snatched up as though it was feeding time at the zoo in front of the restaurant, and Erin spotted Fiona with her crocheted scarves next door.

She blinked the cold-induced tears from her eyes and hugged her blazer tighter around her torso for warmth. "What's up, then?"

"Er…" Frankie worried at her lip and gestured to the chalkboard sign positioned by the doors. "Someone drew… well, you can see what it is."

There was no mistaking the crude image graffitied over Erin's neatly handwritten menu. The joys of working in the centre of Manchester never really did seem to end. "Well… wipe it off."

"That's the problem." Frankie crouched by the sign and picked up a damp cloth hiding in a yellow bucket to demonstrate. The foaming suds had no impact on the drawing. "It won't come off."

"For heavens' sake." Erin's curse remained polite only for the sake of her customers, a few of whom were watching in quiet amusement. "Are you any good at drawing? You could turn it into a…

broccoli, maybe?"

"Nah, that would only work if it wasn't upside down," another voice chimed in, lower and gruffer and closer than Erin had been expecting. She whipped around, her brows furrowing when she found a dark-haired man rocking on his heels behind her. His round features and ruffled curls were slightly familiar, his eyes twinkling with humour. A waiter she had forgotten hiring? But he hadn't followed Erin's all-black dress code, instead wearing a loose, hole-infested knit jumper and sagging denim jeans.

"Why aren't you in uniform?"

"Eh?" His inky eyes danced with amusement, the scruff-covered corner of his mouth quirking upwards.

Erin *definitely* did not remember hiring him. "Wait, did you do this?"

"I can only wish I was so creative." He thrust his hands in his pockets, eyes narrowing until creases began to bunch at the corners. "Sorry... don't I know you?"

Erin was still wondering the same thing. He clearly wasn't a waiter, but he was familiar. And that accent, broad and not belonging to Manchester at all, but rather the Yorkshire Dales where she herself had grown up...

She didn't have time to figure it out either way. She had a penis on her menu and a restaurant full of people inside. "Do you need something, or have you just come to enjoy the exhibition?"

"I'm looking for the manager." He nodded to the Spuds 'n' Puds sign, emblazoned on the red-brick wall in gold lettering.

"You've found her." *Here we go.* A customer complaining that their roast beef was cold after eating it outside in the bloody freezing cold, perhaps, or someone wanting to make it known that her food was too expensive, despite the high quality and skill that went into all of the dishes.

But the man pointed his thumb across his shoulder and said, "I'm the waffle man. Oh, God, don't let that stick. What I mean is I own the waffle truck. You said I could park up here?"

Oh, bollocks. Erin had forgotten that the dessert-themed food truck was arriving today. With a little extra space at the side of her restaurant and no pastry chefs or expertise to provide a dessert menu yet, she'd decided to offer Utter Waffle a place and hopefully bolster her own business in the process.

This, however, was not what she'd had in mind. Brusquely, she nudged past the man to examine the truck. It was... beaten up, to say the least. The once white, now faded yellow paint job was full of scratches and the smell of petrol lingered around in its vicinity: the type of van a mother might warn her children not to get into, even if the dodgy men in it were offering out sweets. The only sign of its function was the striped awning, which was frayed and covered in what looked to be grease stains, and the window beneath. *Utter Waffle* had been plastered on the side doors in uneven, red paint.

"Forgive me, but I was expecting something a bit more... well, professional. It's not very nice to look at, is it?"

"I used it for work when I was a joiner," he said, scratching his neck awkwardly. "Can't afford to buy a proper one yet."

"Yeah, I can see that..."

"Sorry." The weight of his eyes pressed on her again, and she turned around to find him glancing at her quizzically. "Are you sure I don't know you? What'd you say your name was?"

"Erin." Against her better judgement, Erin extended her hand out for him to shake. He did, his skin warm and rough against her frostbitten fingers. "Erin Levine. And you?"

He stiffened suddenly, the colour draining from his face. "Erin. Of course it's you. Jesus. I never expected..." When he noticed Erin's confusion, he clarified: "Sorry. It's me, Rory Peterson. I used to work on your dad's farm way back when."

The name sent a jolt of electricity through Erin, and something else, something she hadn't had to acknowledge for a long time. *Rory*. He'd only been seventeen the last time she'd seen him, all gangly and dotted with hormonal acne. Erin hadn't minded. Fourteen years old and well into her boy band obsession, she was glad of any attention she could get from another teenager.

"Right... I remember. Yes, of course." Her

words came out wooden, forced, as her heart began to pound. Not at the warm memories of chatting to Rory while he wandered around with a wheelbarrow or showing him how to milk Claudia the cow, but at the guilt that had come later. After he'd left. The watching him walk away, heartbroken and betrayed.

She had accused him of stealing her late mother's jewellery, the only thing Erin had had left of her; the only memories she could keep. As a result, Rory had lost his job, lost her trust. Her father kicked him off the farm and told him he was never to return.

She tried to push it all away, schooling her features into their usual stoniness. They were adults now, Erin a professional, and she at least wouldn't have him snooping around her restaurant. Their past would remain in the past, and they would remain separated by two walls.

Rory's uncomfortable laugh sliced through the air between them, forced up from his broad chest. "Wow. It's been a long time. You've changed."

"Well..." Erin smoothed down her blazer and prayed that the heat rising to her face didn't show. "So have you."

He had. His hair had been greasy and short then, the curls that spilt across his forehead now never getting the chance to grow. And he'd filled out since, though not with tough muscle, and the beginnings of a beard shadowed his jaw.

A ghost of a smile curved across his lips, but Erin could see the cool hesitance lingering behind it.

"Anyway, I need to get back to work. Are you all set out here?"

She fidgeted and then scolded herself for it, but she was eager to escape. The less she saw of Rory, the better. He was too much of a reminder. In the difficult few years that had followed Rory's departure, the farmhouse had been left empty, the fields lifeless and overgrown, the furniture re-possessed. Her father had lost everything they'd owned: a gambling addict who had haemorrhaged away every penny to poker games and debt, including Erin's savings. It was one of the reasons she'd worked so hard to get here — so that she'd never feel that hollow nothingness again while staring upon the skeleton of her own home or having to go hungry for days at a time. She relied on herself now. No one else.

"Yep, all good." Rory nodded. "Thanks again for letting me rent out the space. I'll, er, get the permits and paperwork to you once I'm set up."

"Grand." Erin scuttled back into the restaurant before remembering the defaced chalkboard menu. She stepped out again, only becoming more flustered when she realised that the marketgoers were still pointing and laughing at it. Crouching to pick it up was no mean feat while wearing a pencil skirt, but she managed it. That wasn't to say that, with Rory glancing over his shoulder, she wasn't at serious risk of flashing him the red, lacy knickers she wore beneath her tights and skirt.

She'd have to thank Frankie later for leaving it for Erin to deal with; another thing she didn't have the time or patience for today.

Rory thought about getting back into his banged-up food truck and driving away. The last thing he needed was to go about his business beside a restaurant owned by a woman who had once accused him of being a thief. But he needed the space and the money. He wouldn't get another like this now, not when the markets were already open and the stalls all set up. It was either this or go back to that shitty, grey, depressing industrial park, where his only customers were workmen who ordered a bacon butty every morning, knowing full well that Rory only sold sweet breakfasts.

And maybe if he didn't have to sleep there as well, he might have dealt with it. But now that he'd been evicted from his flat, he only had his van, which meant that he never quite stopped smelling of chocolate and grease.

So until he sorted himself out, he'd take what he could get. Even if it was here, with her.

He was midway through scooping out a healthy dollop of ice cream onto a tray of hot cookie dough when Erin emerged from the restaurant a second time that day — with a brand spanking, phallus-free menu listed in handwritten, swirling letters on a clean chalkboard. He had to bow his head in a truck this small anyway to keep from knocking himself out on the ceiling or shelves, but he crouched further and pretended to be focused on his customer's order, his gaze all the while flickering back to her.

She had a ladder in her tights. It spanned from her heel to midway up her calf, a slither of winter-pale skin poking out between the rungs. Still, she surveyed the new menu proudly and smoothed down her skirt, her spine pin-straight. Having spent the majority of his life a joiner and handyman, usually in chatty, relaxed environments, he'd never met anybody who exuded so much bone-chilling authority — the sort where he knew that if she asked him to get down on his hands and knees to polish her shoes, he'd run to find a rag and do it. Or, at least, he'd have to fight not to, if he was feeling more dignified that day.

It was worse because he knew her; worse that those alarmingly blue eyes had once been friendly and familiar. He'd always loved the attention she'd given him on the farm — before she'd made him out to be a ruddy criminal, that was. She'd torn his heart out with that. They'd been friends. They'd laughed together over Sunday roasts and mucked out the pigsty until they were both covered in shit. And now look at them. He more the scruffy toad she'd made him out to feel than ever, jobless, homeless, and hopeless, and she was a bloody restaurant manager whose biggest problem was probably the ripped tights and the graffitied dick.

Stifling a huff, Rory took the customer's money with his most charming smile and wondered where he could park up and sleep tonight. He obviously couldn't stay here. Even if Erin didn't notice, they were near the pubs and soon Manchester would be chock-full of drunkards who'd do far worse than paint a crude drawing onto a chalkboard. He could call his mum...

But his mum worried. Too much. He didn't want her to know what a mess he was, just like his useless dad, who had walked out on them twenty years ago and hadn't bothered with them since. And his sister, who was engaged and pregnant and raking it in with her own hair salon....

He was the embarrassment, the one who just couldn't seem to get by on his own two feet. And he was sick of it. He wouldn't do it. No, he'd make a good go of it here, hopefully with enough profit to get him through the looming winter months and maybe even an apartment deposit. And then he'd answer their calls.

It would be fine. It would all be fine.

Two

Erin raised her eyebrows and tapped the arms of her chair stiffly. Judging by the lopsided, devilish grin Luca sported as he stepped into Erin's office, he was expecting to get lucky. But that wasn't what she'd called him in for today. It seemed the parsley-related telling off this morning hadn't been enough. Mavis had just caught the line chef swapping rosemary for oregano to season the cuts of turkey and beef, and now Erin's body simmered with frustration.

She was sick of being undermined. Sick of Luca acting as though he knew better, trying to adjust recipes she'd inherited from her mother before she'd passed. The point of this restaurant wasn't to be fancy and highbrow. It wasn't to change up flavours. It was to create warm, cosy dishes that tasted of homely Sundays.

"Sit down, Luca," she ordered on a sigh, motioning to the chair opposite.

He did, amusement dancing in his eyes. Was he *laughing* at her? He wouldn't be in a minute. "Yes, ma'am."

She steepled her fingers, staring him down with the steeliest gaze she could muster. "Do you think you know better than me?"

He shrugged. "Depends what we are talking about. Formula 1 racing, yes. Cooking, perhaps. That pink powdery thing you put on your cheeks, not so much."

Erin bit down on her tongue, tasting something bitter. It took every fibre of her not to erupt as heat crawled beneath her skin, up the collar of her shirt, onto her face and into her hairline. She'd never thought Luca a sexist pig before, but here he was, *oink*ing in his sty in front of her.

"*Perhaps*?" she repeated incredulously, choosing to ignore the final insult despite the blow it had dealt. As though her expertise lay in makeup. As though all she was was a walking pot of blusher and not an executive bloody chef. "You think that *perhaps* you might know more about cooking than me?"

A chuckle rumbled from Luca, fringed with all of the practised charm of a man who knew how to dig himself out of very deep holes. Erin was beginning to wonder why she kept handing him the shovel. "Oh, come on. It was a joke. Of course I don't think that."

"So why is it, then, that you've been caught twice today trying to change my recipes behind my back?"

"I'm just trying to put my own spin on the food." He threw out his hands in exasperation, a sandy curl falling into his hazel eyes. He blew it away quickly. "Jesus, Erin, a little bit of parsley isn't doing the customers any harm."

"It's not about the parsley or the customers. It's about the fact that you've repeatedly tried to change things without my consent. You know what those recipes mean to me —"

"I know that they are *five hundred* years old," he interjected. "Don't you think it's time to switch it up? Business is booming, Erin. You could turn this place into something special."

"It already *is* something special!" She jumped to her feet defensively, her fingers flexing at her sides as she scowled down at Luca. Suddenly, she didn't know him at all. Well, she couldn't pretend as though she had ever *really* known him, not down to his roots and bones, but she'd at least trusted him to respect her as a boss and a lover; to see her as his superior when it was necessary. To follow her vision for the restaurant, not the other way around.

Luca sucked in a breath, his sparkle dimming to something flat, something cold. "Erin, darling. The place is called *Spuds 'n' Puds*."

Erin's upper lip curled in contempt. She wouldn't be patronised. She didn't care how many snooty restaurants Luca had worked at: Paris, Milan, Bangkok — they didn't matter. This one was hers, and she loved it as it was. "Do you want to keep your job, Luca?"

He rolled his eyes and hissed out a *pfft*. "What, you're going to fire me?"

"If I have to."

The threat seemed to finally snap him back to attention, a muscle in his jaw ticking as he leaned back in his chair. "Yes. I want to keep this job."

"Good." Erin leaned forward on the desk so that they were on the same eye level, the glossy cherry wood biting into her palms. "Don't *ever* try to patronise me again. My name's not *darling*, it's Erin, and I'm *your* boss, not the other way around. If lines have been blurred with our personal relationship, perhaps it's time to put a stop to it."

His high cheekbones reddened. "Oh, baby. Don't be like that. Perhaps I made a bad decision. I admit. It won't happen again."

"No, it won't."

"I can show you how sorry I am if you'd like." He stood slowly from his chair, leaning into her until only the desk and their heavy breaths pushed between them. She could smell the minty herbs he liked to chew on his breath, the expensive Paco Rabanne cologne on his slightly stubbled neck. And then she was wrapped in it when he inched to close the final bit of distance between them, sealing his lips against her neck, the hinge of her jaw, the back of her ear, slowly, seductively, just as he knew she liked it. Only it didn't feel the way it was supposed to. It didn't ignite fiery lust in her belly. It just left her feeling… wrong. Maybe she couldn't trust Luca anymore. She'd seen something in him she despised today, something that she'd noticed brewing for a few weeks now, in sidelong glares and reports from the kitchen staff.

A rap at the door drew her away, and she tucked an escaping strand of hair behind her ear as someone entered. She could only hope they hadn't seen.

But judging by the way Rory's bashful gaze fell to the floor, she was out of luck. "Sorry, er... I just came with the permit for my truck. I can come back —"

"No, it's fine. Thank you, Luca." She dismissed Luca with a terse nod, not allowing herself to look at him again. She didn't particularly want to.

Luca smirked and turned to leave, but not before looking Rory up and down with far less subtlety than he'd shown when he'd been sneaking forbidden herbs into Erin's recipes. "Who's this? We are hiring the homeless now, but heaven forbid Luca uses parsley?"

Erin's temper spiked again, and she gritted her teeth before replying. "Get out, Luca, before I change my bloody mind and fire you on the spot."

"Yes, ma'am." He saluted Erin and then disappeared, the door swinging shut behind him.

"He's a nice fella'," Rory remarked with raised brows, plonking himself down into the empty chair without permission.

"Yeah, well... he's a good chef," Erin mumbled. She wasn't sure why she was defending Luca now. He certainly didn't deserve it.

"Shame about the personality, then." Rory

passed a small folder across the desk. Erin took it, skimming over the documents. "Permit, rental agreement, deposit... it's all there." When she pursed her lips in surprise, he continued: "Don't look so impressed."

Perhaps Erin *was* slightly impressed. With his slightly dishevelled appearance and the lacklustre food truck parked outside, Rory didn't exactly seem the type to organise his paperwork. Then again, there was a faint smudge of what she hoped was chocolate beneath his signature on the rental agreement. She filed it away in her drawer, allowing herself a small smile. "Fab. Thanks."

"So..." Rory hauled his ankle up to the opposite knee as though they were old friends meeting for coffee and he was just getting comfortable. It was about the strangest thing she'd experienced today, and that was including the penis drawn on her menu and a customer complaining that the iced coffee they'd ordered was too cold.

Erin couldn't help but panic. The last thing she wanted was to rehash the past; chatter away like she hadn't gotten him fired from his summer job. She was a long way away from the girl she'd been in Yorkshire, and so was the rest of her life — and that had been a choice she'd made on purpose. "So?"

"How's the farm? Your dad? Claudia the cow?"

"The farm's gone," she deadpanned, feigning intense interest in the keyboard of her computer.

She'd never noticed before that three-quarters of her name were on the top row. "Not really in touch with my dad. Think we ended up selling Claudia not long after you left."

"Oh." Rory's dark brows drew together in surprise. "What, er... What happened?"

Erin shrugged nonchalantly, though any memory of the farm caused a chasm to open up in her chest, one that threatened to swallow her whole. God, if her mum had been alive to witness it all... "We couldn't afford to run the place anymore. Then I went off to uni and found something better anyway."

"You always were a pro when it came to Sunday dinners." It was true. Sunday roasts were something Erin had always loved to make, taking after her mum. She'd make the Yorkshire puddings and stuffing from scratch — none of that shop-bought Aunt Bessie's rubbish — and the roast potatoes always came out crispy on the outside, fluffy on the inside, full of flavour from the goose fat and seasoning. Rory had always made sure to work late on a Sunday so he could join them, and Erin would always blush when he complimented her cooking, which only spurred her to do it more.

"Well," she said wryly, perhaps a little bit proud that Rory remembered.

"No, really. This place is great. You must be really proud of yourself."

"It took a lot of hard work," Erin admitted, softening just slightly. Maybe they *could* leave the past behind them. Maybe it didn't have to be so uncomfortable. "Anyway… I just wanted you to know that it's all in the past."

Rory scratched his stubbled jaw curiously. "What is?"

"You know. How we left things. I'm sure we've both grown since then, and I'm willing to give you the benefit of the doubt."

His lips twitched. Erin couldn't tell if it was with amusement or anger, and he made no attempt to show her. Instead, a silence fell between them, Rory's shadowy eyes twinkling as though weighing her up. And then he clasped his hands over his stomach and, with a gentle, sardonic scoff, said, "Well, that's mighty big of you, Erin. Generous, too, letting a rehabilitated criminal like me park up outside your restaurant. Cheers."

Flummoxed and perhaps a little bit embarrassed, Erin could only blink and stutter, "I… I just meant…"

"No, I know what you meant." Rory stood up, ruffling a hand through wind-wilted curls. "As long as you're not worried about my sticky fingers being near the cash register, eh?"

He marched out before she could reply, the slammed door causing the walls to rattle. Erin's lids fluttered shut — with regret or irritation, she didn't know. She only knew that she had never expected to see Rory Peterson again, let alone work next to him, and nothing about her past made sense. Nothing about *them* made sense, then or now. Rory had left the farm disgraced and dejected and accused of theft, and now he was here. What was she supposed to do with that?

Clearly, they hadn't left all of it behind them. But if they wanted to work this close to one another, they'd have to push it aside. Erin could do that. She just wasn't sure if Rory could.

Three

Rory managed to survive the rest of his first week parked outside Spuds 'n' Puds without running into Erin too often — and he'd made a fairly decent profit from the influx of customers. In fact, he currently had more money in his cash register than he'd ever had in the truck before, equivalent to at least two weeks' worth of fitting staircases as a joiner. With a renewed hope threatening to kindle in his gut, he set aside the rent he owed Erin and then extra to put towards finding an apartment.

The problem with working in the centre of Manchester was that he couldn't stop noticing all of the people in far worse positions than him. He'd been sleeping in an Asda car park every night, freezing his bollocks off, yes, but there were thousands of people he'd caught wandering around the city with only a sleeping bag to their name. Rory hadn't come from a wealthy family. He knew what it was like to go without a meal or two. In fact, his mother's house had almost been repossessed when his dad had upped and left years ago. He could only imagine how terrifying it must have been to wander around without safe shelter or a hot meal — and in the dead of winter, with the crisp chill crawling deeper into the city by the minute, people without homes would be settling down for another rough night.

And Rory had extra money.

So, he closed up his food truck before the Friday night shoppers poured in and queued up outside the takeaway window for Spuds 'n' Puds, pulling his woollen hat over his ears to protect them from the harsh wind. The woman at the counter looked at him as though he'd gone mad when he reached the front and asked for as many jacket potatoes and trays of cheesy chips as fifty pounds would get him. It was one of the blonde waitresses he'd noticed with Erin on Monday. The name badge pinned to her breast pocket named her Frankie.

"Aren't you the waffle bloke?" she asked while ladling out beans and cheese onto a long line of jacket potatoes.

He grimaced. Apparently, the nickname *had* stuck. "Yep, that's me."

"Weird," she muttered, piling up the polystyrene trays of food and dividing them into three paper bags. "Well, enjoy your spuds."

"Cheers." He gave her the money, apologised to the customers who'd been waiting behind him, and then set off towards Piccadilly gardens, wending his way through crowded, market-lined shopping streets. The mingling smells of sweet incense and smoky hog roasts followed him like a friend, clinging to his coat and making his stomach gurgle. Maybe he should have gotten a meal for himself, too.

The gardens were bustling with just as many people. Commuters spilt onto the pavement, their workweeks done and dusted, and families were already dancing around Primark and Starbucks to stave off the cold. Tram horns bleated, snaking down rusted tracks.

And at the heart of it all, groups and groups of people huddling on benches and outside buildings for warmth, tucked into torn sleeping bags, begging for passersby to spare just a penny.

They needed a good meal, at the very least. Rory knew the feeling. Only now, he had plenty to go around.

$$\infty \infty \infty$$

Erin couldn't help herself. She had to know why one man would need to buy so many trays of jacket potatoes and chips.

Frankie had rushed into the kitchen while Erin had been making her usual afternoon rounds, flustered and flummoxed and claiming that "the waffle bloke has just bought *fifty pounds' worth* of jacket potatoes and chips now we have none left."

Mavis had thrown a fit and was now up to her eyeballs in potato peel while she prepped more for the fryer. "Right before the bloody teatime rush hour, too," she'd muttered — which would actually last until about ten o'clock tonight now, what with the markets being open and it being a Friday. Erin always extended her opening hours over Christmas, a fact that her employees despised.

So, Erin had followed Rory and the three bags of fried and baked spuds through Manchester, the balls of her feet throbbing on their high heels and her breath puffing out like smoke in front of her. Why anyone would subject themselves to so many crowds just for extortionately priced bratwursts and mulled wine was beyond her. Half the shoppers didn't even buy the handmade little gifts on offer at each stall; they just stood in the way to take a few selfies. The novelty had long since worn off for Erin.

Erin was red-faced and in a sour mood by the time they got to Piccadilly gardens. She should have turned back. If she was even slightly sane, she would have turned back when a tall bloke had almost spilt a pint of beer down her shirt. But to have Rory back was strange enough. To have him buy half her supply of potatoes and take them on a walk around Manchester was just plain bizarre.

Well, it was until she understood why. She lingered on the other side of the street in the shadow of an idling tram as Rory crossed over. For an alarming moment, she thought he might be going into Burger King and wondered if he had bigger problems than just their awkward past to contend with. When the tram whistled away, though, and Erin got a decent view, she found that he wasn't heading into the fast-food restaurant at all, but rather crouching down to a man sitting with a dusty old hat in front of him and a solemn Border Collie at his side. An occasional penny or cigarette was dropped at his feet as people passed by.

Rory pulled out a polystyrene tray from one of the bags, and Erin understood. He was giving him a meal.

An elastic string tied around Erin's ribs snapped suddenly. She watched Rory talk to the homeless man before waving him off so he could dig into his chips, sharing them with his dog. And then Rory went to another in the nook of a closed shop before crossing back into the gardens to do the same for a woman hunched on the steps by the water sprinklers.

Why? Rory had abandoned his truck, thrown fifty pounds at Frankie, and gone out of his way to feed people he surely didn't know. Erin passed them every day on her way to work, and the most she ever gave them was a spare bit of change from her purse or a sausage roll from Greggs. Not because she didn't care, but because there was such an overwhelming amount of people living in poverty around Manchester that it felt impossible to help them.

But Rory did. Rory gave them a hot meal, a little bit of kindness. And it reminded her that once, it might have been Erin on these streets, just trying to survive the winter. Dad had made sure that they'd lost everything. The farm, their savings, their home. Erin had escaped by the skin of her teeth, just glad that her student loan had meant she could go to university and stay in campus housing. She'd never gone back home after that, instead staying with her best friend, Rani, outside of term time until she could afford a flat of her own. She'd been so close, though. So close to having nothing at all. If someone had brought around a hot meal on one of her worst days, Erin would have been endlessly appreciative.

Oh, God. How awful she'd been to dredge up her suspicions about Rory the other day. He was a better person than she was, clearly. Erin sighed and crossed over, slumping onto a pigeon-soiled bench without caring about the consequences. She hated herself. And worse still, a part of her still hated Rory for making her confront everything she'd tried to leave behind. With a successful business and a nice apartment, she'd always been able to pretend that the little girl she'd once been, the one left devastated and alone and poor, was someone else entirely. She could file away all of that pain as she would an old delivery invoice, hide it in a locked cabinet where nobody else could get it either.

Nobody but Rory.

Exhaustion weighed on her and an ache began to throb behind her eyes. Erin pinched the bridge of her nose and sucked in a deep breath of air. Mingling spices from the street food market swathed her, a heady reminder of her mistakes.

"Erin?"

Great. Even better that he'd find her here, on the brink of a breakdown after having followed him through Manchester like a bloody stalker. She opened her eyes slowly, delaying the inevitable. Rory towered above her, wreathed in the murky-blue four o'clock sky. Shadows from the looming buildings behind sliced his figure in two, a single ray of golden sunset creeping across his shoulder.

"Hello," she greeted guiltily. "Fancy seeing you here."

"Aye, fancy that." Rory folded his hands into his pockets and rocked on his heels. He must have distributed the rest of the meals while she'd been having an existential crisis on the bench. "Wouldn't happen to be spying on me, would you?"

"No..." Erin shuddered against a brisk gust of wind. In her hurry, she hadn't even put on her scarf or gloves, and her eyes pricked with tears from the icy cold.

"So you just happen to enjoy sitting here, then."

"Maybe I do. Is that a crime?"

Rory rolled his eyes. Defiant dark curls flicked upwards beneath the hem of his hat, his chin dipped into a stripy scarf. "Just seems a coincidence, doesn't it?"

"Alright." Erin stood decidedly, crossing her arms and nodding towards the Starbucks on the corner opposite. If they were going to do this, they'd do it inside. Erin's toes were already turning into blocks of ice. "Coffee?"

"Depends. Are you paying?"

She didn't bother to reply, though of course, it was the least she could do now. Instead, she led him into the cafe, grateful for the cloak of coffee-laced warmth. She could feel Rory behind her, shifting from foot to foot as she scanned the menu printed on the wall.

"Tea? Coffee?" she asked over the shrill whir of a blender behind the till.

"Tea's fine."

Erin ordered a cappuccino for herself as well as Rory's tea, and they managed to hop onto a table in the corner that had only just been abandoned. Like everywhere else at Christmas, the place was overcrowded and noisy.

She sat down, clearing her throat. Rory hovered above his own chair for a moment as though deciding whether to stay or leave. A twinge of guilt needled through her as she cupped her numb hands around her mug. Had it come to this? Could he not even sit at a table with her?

"Ants in your pants?"

Finally, Rory sat, the chair legs scraping across the floor. "I suppose I'm just wondering what I'll be accused of this time. Why did you follow me?"

She tapped a manicured fingernail against the rim of her mug, deciding how best to approach this. But they couldn't keep dancing around each other. Erin rarely withheld the truth from anyone.

In fact, she usually used quite the opposite strategy, and it often landed her in trouble. "Frankie told me you'd bought a suspicious amount of food. I thought it highly unlikely that you had enough friends to share it with. Maybe I was curious."

"Probably thought I was trafficking jacket potatoes." He sipped his tea, eyes flashing towards the window as though he couldn't look at her. And perhaps it hurt Erin. Perhaps a part of her was just a fourteen-year-old girl who had found an unlikely friendship in the farmhand. "Or maybe I'd just go and throw them at kids' heads for the sake of it, because I'm an untrustworthy, unpredictable criminal."

"Oh, Rory…" Erin muttered impatiently. "It's not like that. God."

"Oh, have I been graced with the benefit of the doubt again, then?"

"I was *fourteen years old.*" Her words came out terse; scathing. "Something valuable went missing from my room. What was I supposed to think?"

"We were *friends.*"

Erin thought of the friends she'd had at that age. People who used her as the butt of the joke and then abandoned her when she fell into poverty. And then there was her father, the one man she was supposed to trust, to care for her.

"Friendship doesn't mean anything." She'd found that out the hard way.

Rory's lips parted in surprise, a line creasing

between his brows. "Bit cynical, isn't it?"

Was it cynical? It didn't feel cynical. It felt realistic. Erin couldn't rely on the people she loved. In the end, everyone was out for themselves, driven by selfish desires. It was why so many people were on the streets. It was why Erin had lost so much.

She couldn't say any of this, so she gazed absently outside the window instead, trying to keep herself separate from the conversation, just like she always did. She didn't want Rory's eyes to keep boring into her like that. She didn't want him to plant that seed of doubt again; didn't want to admit that afterwards, she hadn't been sure if Rory really had been the perpetrator. He hadn't been the only person in that house who would have found use in the jewellery.

"I didn't steal your mother's jewellery, Erin," Rory mumbled, more delicately than Erin could have ever deserved. "I think you know that. I think you always knew that."

"I wouldn't have…" She broke off, taking a deep breath to steel herself. Did she have to be so bloody fragile? "I wouldn't have accused you if I didn't think it was you."

"And now?"

"Now what?" She forced herself to return his focus, her throat bobbing as she swallowed.

Rory's tongue swept across his bottom lip carefully. "Now, do you still think it was me?"

"Does it matter?" she whispered.

He motioned between them as though to say, *look at us; look at the rift you're causing, even now.* "Clearly, it does."

Erin would sooner disappear than admit the truth; that not long after Rory had left, she'd wound up bankrupt and hungry, all of her savings wiped from her bank account. She'd started working in a tearoom not long after, and most of those earnings had somehow found their way into Dad's hands, too. Maybe Rory hadn't been the one who had betrayed her, stolen from her, but the alternative... that Dad would be so lost to his addiction that he'd sell Mum's things or use them as stakes...

The very idea made her feel sick to her stomach. It would be the final nail in the coffin.

She pushed the coffee away, a lump gathering in her throat. "I don't know."

Rory tutted and shook his head, making to leave. It wasn't fair. Erin knew it wasn't fair.

So she spoke up. "No. No, Rory, I don't think it was you."

He stilled, waiting expectantly.

Erin's lids shuttered, the din of the coffee shop shut out until there was nothing but the blood pounding in her ears. "Did you know about my dad's problems?"

"Yes, I knew."

It made sense. Rory had been older than her. He'd seen Dad head out every weekend, leaving just the two of them. Two kids on a farm. That had to be some sort of health and safety hazard in itself. Still, Erin had enjoyed Rory's presence so much that she hadn't minded, hadn't paid attention. She should have. She should have run away before it ever got so bad. Maybe she should have left with Rory.

"That jewellery was all I had left of my mum," she admitted shakily. "I didn't want to believe that... I couldn't ever..."

"I know. I get it." Rory's hand found hers across the table, warm and calloused and too much for her to handle. She didn't deserve his understanding, so she snatched herself away, pretending that she had an itch below her dimpled chin.

Understanding, Rory leaned back and sipped his tea. Erin wished he wouldn't keep looking at her as though he knew her. As though he was waiting for something. Something more than she could give. An apology, perhaps.

"Look." He cleared his throat and readjusted his hat, his knee jiggling beneath the table. "It's in the past, eh? We were both young. We had no idea what we were doing."

Erin clung to the olive branch for all it was worth, though she should have been the one offering it. "Agreed." She tilted her head, catching sight of one of the women Rory had offered a meal to chowing down on her jacket potato in the doorway of an empty hairdresser's outside. "Did they enjoy the food?"

"No. They said it was terrible. Tastes like shite."

A surprised laugh bubbled from Erin, and the toe of her shoe nudged against his shin. "You did a good thing for them."

"Well…" His cheek dimpled with a lopsidedly bashful grin. "I'd hope that if it were me, someone would do the same."

Me too, Erin wanted to agree, but stopped herself. When it had been her, nobody had done anything to help, not even her dad. She wondered, just for a second, if things might have been different if Rory hadn't left the farm. If he'd have been there when everything had turned to dust.

But it didn't matter. She didn't need a man who thought himself a saviour. She'd been her own saviour, pulled herself out of the rubble all on her own, and she was stronger for it. Cynical and cold and maybe a bit lonely, but stronger.

Strong enough to walk out of the cafe with him a little bit later and pretend as though there weren't still scars shared between them.

Four

Erin didn't realise how late it was until her tired eyes dragged from the Spuds 'n' Puds website she was in the middle of updating to today's date in the corner of her computer screen. She hadn't even noticed that night had flooded the office with shadows, only the silvery light of the screen limning her face.

Everyone else had left the restaurant hours ago, just like Erin should have. Somehow, though, she never seemed to get enough done when she had twenty-odd staff to deal with and a steady stream of customers to attend to. Of course, that meant that she overcompensated with late hours, headaches, and a furiously rumbling stomach.

She shook her head and closed the computer down. Experience had proved that if she carried on much longer, she'd be dozing on her keyboard until dawn, and her spine protested against that thought. She needed her own bed tonight; needed to at least try to get some sleep.

Still, when she locked up and saw that Rory's truck was still parked outside, she couldn't help herself. There was one last bit of work she could do, and it would save her a job tomorrow. Wrapped in the sweet scent of fresh waffles, Erin knocked on the back door of the Utter Waffle food truck, warily eyeing a couple of drunk men stumbling past as she did.

Thankfully, she didn't have to wait long. The door creaked open a moment later. Rory greeted her with a bowed head and hunched shoulders — he was too tall for such a small van.

Surprise crossed his features, and Erin had expected as much. They hadn't spoken since the coffee and revelations last week, and Erin might have kept it that way had she not needed his assistance now.

"Hi. Sorry it's late." It was freezing, too. Erin rubbed her hands together and invited herself into the van, partly because she was desperate for the small bit of warmth and partly because she was curious to see what it was like inside.

Rory stepped aside — not that he had much choice — and shut the door behind them. "Er, hello?"

The interior of the truck wasn't much more pleasant than the exterior. The countertops were a few heavy plates away from crumbling, and Erin dared not touch them in case it took less than that. The walls were a cold, steam-mottled metal and the shelves had been organised haphazardly. Erin tutted apprehensively. Chocolate sauce next to antibacterial gel could make for a terrible mistake and a hefty lawsuit.

In fact, she wondered how Rory had managed to get his food hygiene license at all. She could still smell oil and dust from the old tools it must have contained before.

She stilled only when she glimpsed a heap of blankets and pillows atop a large duffel bag, stacked in the corner as though recently used.

He wasn't… He wasn't *sleeping* here, was he?

She could understand why he'd need bedding and belongings if he was on the road, but he was here until the markets closed on Christmas Eve. Surely he had *somewhere* to stay until then.

She tried to ignore it. It wasn't her place, and she wasn't here to pry. "I just came to ask if you had any menus going spare. I'm in the process of adding your information onto our social media and website so that customers know that we have a dessert truck next door. Good for business and all that."

"Right…" Rory frowned and rattled through a drawer, pulling out a flimsy, plain pamphlet. There was no logo, no drawings or images, just a simple list of the food on offer with their slightly underpriced cost. Clearly, he hadn't gotten the memo that people would splash a tenner out on any old dish at the markets as long as it was Instagrammable. "Here you go."

"Thanks. Is your social media on here as well?"

"Oh, I'm no good with Twitter and all that. I'm not really online."

"You run a business and you're not online?"

Erin arched an eyebrow. It was a miracle he'd survived this long.

Rory shrugged. "Don't have time to figure it out."

"Well, if I were you, I'd find some. You might be doing well now, but once Christmas is over with, people are going to forget you exist unless you remind them."

"I'm doing alright." He clenched his jaw, seeming to grow taller, tenser. "You're not the only person who knows how to run a business."

"Is that why you're sleeping in a beaten up food truck?" The words slipped out before Erin could stop them, her defensiveness spurred on by his. She tucked her chin to her chest with shame, wishing she could take it back. But they were out there now, hanging like a sword between them, and she couldn't look past it to face him. "Sorry. That's none of my business. I just… I saw the blankets, and I assumed."

Rory loosed a ragged, drawn-out sigh and scraped his curls back irritably. Erin forced herself to lock eyes with him and then wished she hadn't. His were blazing and… sombre. Lost. Anger, she had been prepared for, but she wasn't sure she could handle the disappointment or the loneliness there. As though he'd expected more from her.

And he should have. If anybody knew what it was like to struggle, it was her.

"It's temporary," he muttered finally. "I'm saving up for a flat deposit."

Erin's focus flickered back to the tatty blankets and pancake-flat pillows. What now? Would she walk out, go home to her nice, warm apartment? Pretend that she didn't know Rory would be sleeping in here while she curled up on a double memory foam mattress? Did he even have a heater to keep warm? She couldn't see one.

"Just... think about the social media thing," she said. "I can help you set it all up if you want."

Rory nodded. "Will do."

She should have left then, but she wasn't that person, and she didn't want to be. She remembered what it had felt like to sleep on a cold floor; remembered wishing that she could feel safe again, because a roof over her head hadn't been enough when the house had been emptied by debt collectors and her things were all gone.

And Rory had spent his own money feeding people with less than him just last week, despite the fact he was living in his food truck. It wasn't right. Nobody deserved that. Erin hadn't. Rory didn't. The people he'd fed didn't either, but Erin could only do something for one person now. The pain of that life, the refusal to ever go back to it, made the decision for her.

"I have a couch going spare. It's not much, but it's comfier than here, I'd imagine. Warmer, at least."

Rory's forehead wrinkled with lines, and he blinked in disbelief. "I appreciate the offer, but I'm not your charity case, Erin."

"It isn't charity. It's…" She sighed, twizzling one of her coat buttons around on a loose piece of thread. "I suppose it's an apology. A delayed one."

"You don't owe me —"

"Fine," she cut off quickly. "Then it's a favour from an old friend."

Erin didn't know if she had a right to call herself a friend. She only knew that if she left Rory here tonight, she wouldn't be able to sleep. Uneasiness was already stirring in her gut, so much like what she used to feel when she'd watched her world disappear piece by piece, penny by penny. She'd do it for anyone, she told herself, and hoped it was true.

Rory's eyes narrowed. "It's really not necessary."

"I know. But I would like to think if it were me, someone would do the same." They were an echo of his words, spoken in Starbucks last week, but somehow they felt like hers, too.

He responded with a thin smile, a subtle nod, an understanding they'd never quite shown one another before. "Okay. Thank you."

Relief flooded through Erin, and something else, something strange and warm and prickly. Something that reminded her of the farm, of sunshine-drenched weekends, of laughter in an echoey barn.

"Good," was all she said. "You can follow me home, then."

∞ ∞ ∞

Rory hadn't thought this through. He realised that about one second after stepping foot in Erin's apartment, when he burst into an Irish jig on the welcome mat to make sure his scruffy work boots were clean enough for the pristine carpet.

To be fair, he'd been expecting her to live in one of those flashy new highrise buildings by Victoria Station that most people who had grown up in the north probably couldn't afford. But they ended up well outside of the city centre in Ashton-under-Lyne, the red-bricked buildings overlooking a canal. It was peaceful, at least, and Rory had managed to find a spot to park outside.

Still, he didn't belong... *here*. The place was spotless, as though Erin didn't actually live here at all — and judging by the hours she worked, she probably didn't. He would be sullying her nice velvet couch by sleeping on it; would be a splotch of dirt in an otherwise perfectly sparkling home.

"Are you sure —?"

"Yes," Erin said before he'd even gotten the question out. She set down her bag and keys, flicking on the kettle.

"It's a nice place." Rory tried to ease into it, shoving his hands in his pockets so he wouldn't be tempted to touch the photographs on the walls or the ornaments on the tables. They were all art or pictures with friends. None of Erin's dad, or the Italian bloke she worked with, who seemed a little too familiar with her to just be a co-worker.

But not familiar enough to be hanging on her wall. He didn't know why that mattered.

"It's alright for sleeping in." She shrugged, a tired smile curling across her lips as she placed down two mugs. "I'm not here enough to use it for much else."

Driving home, almost every house or apartment or shopfront they'd passed had been lit with Christmas lights or a tree, or had at least glistened with a bit of tinsel. There were no such things in here. It was like a showhouse. "No time for decorations this year?"

"Ugh." Erin rolled her eyes, the kettle's steam curling around her as it bubbled to a boil. "I don't do Christmas."

He raised his brows, halting his inspection to gawp at her in surprise. "*What*? Don't tell me you're a Scrooge."

"Bah humbug," Erin deadpanned, eyes lowered as she poured water into the mugs. "Milk?"

"Just a drop." And then, because Rory couldn't just let it go: "How can't you like Christmas? I'm bloody broke and homeless, and even I have a few bits of tinsel around the truck."

"Yeah, well…" Her voice lowered as she wandered over to the fridge to retrieve the milk. Green-labelled, semi-skimmed, Rory noted with distaste.

Might as well have just used water instead. A farmer's daughter should have known better.

"Well?" he urged, bracing his elbows against the counter as she brought him his tea.

She sighed, looping her fingers through the handle of her own mug and kicking off her high heels. It left her just about eye level with him while he was hunched over; made her look smaller in more ways than just height. He hadn't really seen the old Erin since meeting the new one. *His* Erin had been young, innocent, doe-eyed, always giggling and poking fun out of him. This one was focused, driven, a businesswoman who never paused for breath.

Only now, just for a moment, she had. Fatigue left her shoulders sagging, and dark circles emerged beneath day-old makeup under her eyes. And yet somehow, with her features softer and her guards lowered, he glimpsed the girl he'd known on the farm. The one who could just sit with him, talk to him. It felt as though no time had passed at all.

"I suppose Christmas loses its magic a bit after you've spent a few sitting on the floor of an empty farmhouse, eating stale bread and butter," she admitted finally, her gaze piercing yet not quite directed at him.

Rory frowned, his heart thundering in his chest. He hadn't known. How could he have known? "The farm got that bad?"

"Worse." Her voice cracked, just slightly.

Rory wouldn't have noticed if he hadn't been searching for it. And then she cleared her throat and sipped her tea, another woman altogether. It didn't fool him. He still saw the way she had to bite down on her lip to keep it from wobbling. "Anyway, all I asked for that year, the one after you left, was a tree. Me and Mum used to go shopping for one and decorate it together before she died. It didn't feel right not to. But we couldn't afford one. The place was about to get repossessed. Most of our things had been sold or taken or pawned. I ended up cutting down one of the pines in the back garden." A small smile, as though the memory was pleasant rather than devastating. "Nearly lost a finger, to be honest. So... no. I don't really do decorations anymore."

"I'm sorry, Erin." Rory's fingers curled into his palms so that he wouldn't be tempted to reach out. "I can't imagine..."

He couldn't. If things ever got that bad, he had his mum, his sister. But the only person there to take care of Erin had been the one to put her in that situation. Rory remembered watching it; seeing Thomas, her father, "just nip out" for five hours at a time and come back with the glum features of a man who had just sold another part of himself.

"Anyway," Erin's sharp intake of breath sliced away whatever moment, whatever candour, had come between them, "are you hungry?"

"No. No, I'm good. Thank you."

"Well, if you need a shower or anything,

the bathroom's through the hall. I'll get the couch made up for you."

She abandoned her tea, avoiding his gaze as she padded past him into the hallway. After the opening and shutting of a cupboard door, she returned with a pile of pillows and blankets, setting them down on the couch. He could smell the lavender detergent on them from here and relaxed without meaning to. "You're welcome to anything in the kitchen, and I never use the TV, so you might as well."

"Thank you..." He shifted, uneasy. Though he'd said himself that he'd want someone to help him out, he didn't quite like accepting other people's generosity when it came down to it. He felt like a burden, a shadow in her living room, a pathetic charity case. What must she think of him? "I'll start looking for a flat tomorrow and hopefully be out of your hair as soon as possible."

"There's no rush, honestly. Take as long as you need."

Not quite sure how else to express his gratitude, Rory smiled at her, his restless fingertips tapping a silent beat against his thigh.

Erin smoothed down the sheets a final time. "I, er... I was thinking about last week. About what you did, buying food for people going hungry."

"Hmm?" Rory hummed, modesty leaving him bashful.

"I thought maybe I'd join you next time. A few times a week. The restaurant isn't doing as much as it should be for the homeless, and I want to change that."

He softened. Every time he thought he knew her, she changed his mind again. She reminded him of one of those penny sweets he used to get from the post office after school as a kid — a chocolate lime. Sour and hard-boiled on the outside, soft and sweet in the middle. Worth tearing through the bad to get to the good. "It sounds like a plan then."

Erin tugged at the hem of her shirt as though unsure. "Good. Okay. Night, then."

"Night."

Once she'd left, he sank down onto the couch with his head in his hands. He didn't know what he was doing; didn't know how he'd gotten here. He only knew that Erin's dimly-lit living room and soft couch were a thousand times better than a cold night spent on the floor of his truck, or waking up smelling of the same grease he'd fallen asleep with.

Maybe it was time to put his pride aside and let himself be helped. He had just never expected Erin Levine to be the one to crack him.

Five

Erin hadn't lived with a man since the farm with her dad, but it was surprisingly easier than expected. She woke the following morning and stumbled into the kitchen to a cup of coffee and a full English breakfast, the bacon crisp and smoky just as she liked it and the coffee black. "To say thanks," Rory had claimed uncomfortably before digging into his own plate.

He'd folded all his sheets from the couch, too, and had only taken five minutes in the shower. He hadn't left the toilet seat up like Erin's married friends complained about constantly. As far as guests went, hers wasn't bad at all. And if she had found her gaze lingering a little bit too long on Rory's soft, protruding stomach and broad, hair-smattered chest when he'd emerged from the bathroom still buttoning up his shirt... well, that was just her trying to adjust her image of Rory in her brain. She still saw him as an awkward teenager, after all. Adult him was something she was still getting used to.

She didn't tell Luca about Rory when she kissed him good morning later that day. Luca wouldn't understand. He came from a well-off family, born with a silver spoon in his mouth, and to him, Yorkshire was just a type of pudding rather than the place both Erin and Rory had grown up in with money an ever-present worry niggling through their lives. Erin had never told him about the farm or her dad, either. In fact, they rarely talked about anything other than the restaurant. Their relationship was more lust than anything else and always had been. Erin was fine with keeping it that way.

When Erin emerged from the restaurant early that evening, Rory's truck was already gone. She didn't blame him, either. They'd shut up two hours before closing time themselves. The unpredictable British weather had been slipping between hailstone and rain all day, leaving the markets damp, dreary, and empty. It was back to rain now, the type that dragged its icy claws down Erin's face and through her clothes. She used her blazer to protect herself from it as she sprinted to her car, teeth chattering and curse words escaping from her mouth.

She'd expected to find Rory already home when she got there, but her apartment was empty. Kicking off her shoes and traipsing puddles into her hallway, she took the opportunity to have a long, hot shower, not even bothering to scrub off her makeup first. She was exhausted. Rundown, if she was being honest with herself. She loved running a business, but she rarely had free time to relax now, and she usually used any she did to catch up with paperwork and bills anyway. It was easier to keep busy, especially over Christmas.

It wasn't until she forced herself to turn the shower off and stepped out, dripping, onto her fluffy bathmat that she realised she hadn't brought in a towel. She'd been so freezing, so desperate, that she hadn't even thought before flinging off her soggy clothes and getting in.

"Rory?" she shouted, just in case, though she was sure she would have heard the door if he had come in in the last twenty minutes.

Only silence was her answer. With a sigh of relief, Erin opened the bathroom door and peeked out her head. Empty. She slid out into the hall and covered her body with her hands as best she could, the cool air hitting her bare, damp skin.

Except, when Erin slinked down the corridor and reached her own bedroom door, the front door opened, revealing... a very skeletal, lopsided tree with legs. The legs were Rory's, she realised, and he was poking his head between two branches.

"Oh, fuck!" Erin grappled with the handle of her door, but her wet hands were too slippery to grip it. "Don't look! Don't look!"

"What — *shit!*" From the corner of her eye, she saw Rory spin around still holding the tree, leaving his back turned to her. The front door fell shut behind him with enough force that it might have left cracks in the walls. Erin wished it had. She wished the whole building would crumble with her in it, because she knew that he had had time to see her before she'd told him to look away. In fact, she could still feel the ghost of his gaze licking a line of flames down her body.

"Why are you naked?" Rory asked.

"Why are you carrying a dead tree?" Erin snapped fiercely, finally managing to open her door and slip inside. She slammed it closed behind her and turned the lock for good measure, her head dropping to her hands.

Idiot. Silly, naked idiot. Oh, God. Had he seen anything? What had he seen? How much? Not her boobs, she hoped, though she was certain she'd been covering them. But then that meant she hadn't really been paying attention to the lower part, and she hadn't had a good wax in a while, and besides that, there were her overflowing love handles and the pink and white stretch marks on her thighs and the alien tattoo she'd gotten after a few too many Jägerbombs, when Dana Scully had become her bisexual awakening.

Erin wanted to shrivel up and die. But she wasn't supposed to be *that* girl anymore. She wasn't supposed to be self-conscious. She was a restaurant manager, an executive chef, and if well-toned, very attractive Luca could see her body, anybody could. It was a bit different when she'd known the man since the age of fourteen, and had sported a rather big crush on him, though. A little bit more difficult to remind herself that she was an adult and so was he, and it was just her body, just her boobs, just her bare arse.

"Look, I'm sorry!" Rory shouted, his voice closer now. He must have been standing in the corridor. "I didn't know you were a nudist is all."

"I'm not a nudist, for Christ's sake," she hissed. "Did you see anything?"

"Nope, nothing. Promise." His words might have meant more if they weren't broken up by bubbling laughter. "Was that a tattoo on your left arsecheek?"

Erin narrowed her eyes as though they might shoot lasers through the door. "You said you didn't see anything! *Liar!*"

"No, I didn't. Only the tattoo, and you moved so quickly I couldn't make it out." And then a loud chuckle just to prove it. "Look, I really am sorry. I am. And I've got something for you out here."

"I saw it. A dead tree. Why did you get me a dead tree?" She huffed, searching finally for some clothes. Her fingers trembled as she rooted through her drawers, settling on a pair of leggings and a loose, turtleneck jumper. If she dressed conservatively enough now, maybe it would cancel out the things Rory had just seen.

"It's not a dead tree. Just come and have a look."

The last thing Erin wanted was to emerge from her room again and see him. But locking herself in forever would be childish, and Erin wasn't a child. She was a successful businesswoman, she reminded herself, and she did have quite good calves from walking in heels all day. Maybe between them and the tattoo, they were distracting enough that Rory didn't see anything else.

With a deep breath, she finally unlocked her door and stepped out, wandering into the living room with her fluffiest socks on. Rory sat on the couch, trying to suppress an amused smirk without much luck. His high cheekbones were flushed pink. "Hello."

"*Don't.*" She refused to meet his gaze, instead crossing her arms and dragging down the hem of her jumper as though he still had X-ray vision.

"Oh, come on. It's funny."

"Hilarious," she deadpanned, turning her focus to the dead tree moulting pine needles in the centre of her living room. "What's this, then?"

"A Christmas tree!" Brightening, Rory stood and adjusted a few of the most bent branches.

"Thought Christmas trees were supposed to be green."

"Well, I couldn't afford a fancy one. This one was the cheapest I could find. Bargain, if you ask me."

She raised an eyebrow and meandered her way around both the tree and the pouffe to find her hairbrush. It was plonked on the windowsill, where she'd left it in a rush this morning — and every other morning since the day she'd moved in. "I told you I don't do Christmas trees."

"Yeah, but that's rubbish, Erin." He petted the tree as though it was his new best friend. "You can't spend the rest of your life without Christmas decorations because of a bad memory. You have to reinvent it. Reclaim it for yourself. You have your own apartment now, your own business. You're not fifteen anymore, and you deserve to remind yourself of that."

"With a dead tree?" Despite her sarcasm, his words took her aback. She couldn't remember the last time anybody had acted this way for her. Rory had gone out of his way to spend money he didn't have on something to help Erin? Why? She didn't really deserve it, not after the mistakes she'd made with him.

"It's not dead," he repeated impatiently.

"Well, it's making a mess of my carpet."

"It's part of the charm. I got a tree skirt anyway, and a few other bits from my mum's house. She was going to chuck them. I rescued them from the bin." He gestured to a bag on the couch. Curiosity getting the better of her, Erin poked her nose in. The decorations smelled musty and old, but they sparkled and caught the light, a rainbow of colours and a tangle of tinsel. And maybe her heart did flutter just a little bit.

Not that she would show it.

Instead, she combed through her hair and then tucked it behind her ears, eyeing the tree a final time. Maybe it *was* time to move on from life at the farm. It wasn't as though she had a choice now: the tree was here, and no garden centre in their right mind would take this one back. "Alright. Fine. But you're doing all the decorating."

"Nope. We're doing it together. We're going to stick on some festive music and do this the proper way."

"You've been staying here one day and you've taken over my flat."

"I'm spreading Christmas cheer!" he defended, pulling out his phone. Erin couldn't help but notice that it was an ancient model of Samsung, scuffed on every edge and about as close to falling apart as the tree. A moment later, Wham!'s 'Last Christmas' drifted from it, tinny and crackling. Rory placed the phone on the arm of the couch and then decided to sing, too. It might have been the cheesiest thing Erin had ever witnessed, but her lips quivered with a smile she tried to trap.

Defeated, she began rooting through the bag of decorations, pulling out a golden piece of tinsel. "So you went to see your mum?"

"Yeah... about that... " Rory took out a handful of baubles and began stringing them on the branches haphazardly. "I, er, might have let slip that I'm staying here."

Erin frowned in confusion. "So?"

"Well, they decided to invite themselves over for tea next week. I hate it when my mum worries about me so I never told her that I'd been evicted from my last place."

"She didn't know you were living in your truck?"

Rory shook his head. "She would have made me come home, and her place is small enough as it is… It was just easier if she didn't know."

"Okay…" Erin pondered this a moment, trying to block out George Michael's wistful notes. Nobody had ever come around for tea before, except Luca, of course, and maybe the occasional friend. But families? Erin didn't even know what a family was anymore. "It's no problem, Rory. Your family is more than welcome here. If you let me know the day, I'll get out of your hair, and then you won't have to tell her you're sleeping on the couch."

"Oh, you wouldn't have to —"

"It's no problem. Really." She smiled reassuringly, glancing at him. The distraction meant that when she went to swathe the tree in tinsel, she accidentally brushed Rory's outstretched hand. Her skin tingled with warmth and surprise, more so when neither one of them moved away or acknowledged it.

A knock at the door tugged them apart. Erin swallowed whatever it was she'd felt and went to answer it, dread curdling in her gut when she was met with Luca's wide, white-teethed grin.

"Surprise!" He pulled up a paper bag labelled 'Monaldo's' — Erin's least favourite Italian restaurant. They used so much garlic that she always ended up with a stomach ache for days afterwards. "I brought your favourite."

Your *favourite*, she almost corrected, but she was more concerned by the line forming between Luca's brows when he looked over her shoulder.

"What's the waffle man doing here?"

"I, er, I can go…" Rory began, but Erin held her hand up to stop him quickly.

"No, no. It's okay." And then to Luca: "Rory is actually staying on the couch until he finds a new place to live."

"A homeless man is sleeping on your couch and you didn't think to tell me?"

Anger spiked in her. "Rory is an old friend. I don't need your permission to help him out."

"An old friend, is he?" Luca glanced between them scathingly, his fingers clenched into fists at his side. "You've never been interested in charity work before, Erin."

Erin sucked in a sharp breath. Not only was it another disgusting dig at Rory, but it was also a lie. Erin had held plenty of fundraisers over the years for all sorts of local Manchester charities. She opened her doors for Pride every year. She collaborated with women's charities and donated old equipment to cookery schools. Luca wouldn't know because he never bothered to help out. Whatever snooty, capitalist, parsley-obsessed establishment he thought she was running, he was wrong. In her blazing fury, all she could grind out was: "*Excuse* me?"

"I really think I'll go —"

"Sit down, Rory!" Erin bit out, and then instantly regretted it. She wasn't supposed to be yelling at Rory. Her problem lay with Luca, her boyfriend — and he wouldn't be that for very much longer. "Get out, Luca."

Luca's eyes widened incredulously. "You're kicking *me* out?"

"Yes. You're pissing me off." She began ushering him to the door, aware of Rory's gaze burning into her back. "You know, you don't have to be a twat every day. You can take the night off."

"Oh, come on." His accent thickened as though he thought it might earn him some favours. As though Erin was that easily manipulated. "You're acting ridiculous."

"You're acting like an entitled prat. And, by the way, I don't even like Monaldo's, and I've told you that more than enough times." She reached past him to open the door, shoving the bags of food into his arms. "Goodbye."

"But —"

Erin shut the door on his argument, too exhausted to hear any more of it. Maybe she was being cruel, but Luca was crueller, trying to put Rory down the way he did. It wasn't right, and Erin would never be the type of woman to sit back and watch. Not with Rory or anyone else. Things with Luca had been fun and new and different, mostly because they'd had so much sex that they didn't have to talk to one another. Now he'd opened his mouth, she was repulsed.

Ashamed that Rory had witnessed it all, and worse, that she'd shouted at him, she turned around with her head bowed. "Sorry for shouting at you. It was him I was angry with. He shouldn't talk to you like that."

Rory shrugged and went back to hanging baubles on the tree. "S'Okay."

"No, it's not," Erin said firmly.

"Then why are you with him?" Rory turned back to her, eyes sharpening with the challenge. "I didn't think someone like that would be your type."

Erin only realised she didn't have an answer when she opened her mouth and no words came out. She scraped back her damp hair in frustration and collapsed onto the couch, noticing only then that Christmas songs were still playing on Rory's phone. "It wasn't serious or anything. We never really talked, so I didn't know he… I didn't know he was so up his own arse. And then he started putting parsley in my gravy and it all made sense."

"Parsley in your gravy?" Rory wrinkled his nose. "Is that a euphemism?"

She batted his joke away with her hand. "He's started changing my recipes. Undermining me at work. Taking charge of my staff like he runs the place and not me. God, I think I might hate him a little bit, actually."

He chuckled. "Me too, funnily enough."

"Sorry," she said again, blinking up at him as something strange, something aching, clogged her throat. She'd made a mess; chosen a man who was completely and utterly repugnant and went against everything she believed in. And for what? An Italian accent and washboard abs? She should have been better than that. She should have seen it sooner. Maybe she'd just been so surprised that somebody like him could want someone like her.

Rory sighed and sat down beside her, tapping her knee gently. "You don't need to apologise on his behalf."

"I'm apologising on *my* behalf."

"Erin..." His brows knitted together, his throat bobbing beneath a shadow of dark stubble: strained, as though he was wrestling with whether or not to say something. Erin rarely had that problem. She usually tended to say whatever it was she thought, and that was why she'd just shoved Luca out of her apartment without warning him. "You deserve better than him, y'know?"

She didn't know if it was the truth. She didn't know if dating somebody like Luca made her just as bad. She didn't know if she'd changed too much; if, in her effort to run from the farm and poverty, she'd reduced herself down to a workaholic city girl who had forgotten how to laugh. When was the last time she'd laughed?

Decisively, she locked eyes with Rory. "Turn this shite music off, Rory. If we're going to listen to Christmas songs, you have to put on Mariah Carey."

"That's more like it." He grinned and obeyed, picking up his phone. A moment later, the opening notes of 'All I Want for Christmas is You' rang out. "I knew I'd change your mind."

"I don't know what you mean." Even as she

said it, she pulled out an elf hat from Rory's bag and, despite the dust and damp smell clinging to it, placed it on her head. She plonked a sparkly red Santa-style one embroidered with the words 'I've been naughty' on Rory and then returned to decorating the tree.

It was strange to have so much life and music fill her apartment. Strange to be decorating it and laughing and singing. Strange, but good. Maybe it was time for change.

Six

Erin had managed to avoid Luca outside of work hours since the argument, and he seemed to be doing the same — until she got back from a meeting with the bank the following Wednesday and found that Spuds 'n' Puds were now offering a soup of the day. Carrot and coriander.

Erin had never put soup on the menu in her life. In fact, the last thing she'd ever have the restaurant sell was *soup*. She *hated* soup, and she especially hated coriander.

"Frankie," she snapped at the waitress closest, pulling her aside from where she'd been checking up on a table. She pointed at the chalkboard menu accusingly, lowering her voice only for the sake of the customers. "What is *that*?"

Frankie blinked in confusion, wide-eyed and skittish. "Er, that's the menu."

Erin inhaled through her nose steadily, her eyes fluttering shut as she counted the last threads of her patience. *Give me strength.* "Yes, I know it's the menu. Why does it say that we're serving soup? *Have* you been serving soup today?"

Frankie shrugged, sweat beginning to glisten in her hairline. "Yes, but Luca said it was your idea."

Luca. Of course it was bloody Luca. Nobody else would have dared tamper with Erin and her menu. "When you get a minute, grab a cloth and wipe that down. The menu hasn't changed. Spuds 'n' Puds does not serve *soup,* and nobody changes that but me."

She marched off into the kitchen before Frankie could reply, thrusting the double doors open. Her staff jumped in surprise when they both slammed shut at the same time. "Luca! My fucking office. *Now!*"

Without waiting, she continued on into the corridor, stepping into her office and standing stiff-spined behind her desk. Luca slinked in a moment later, his jaw clenched and defiance blazing in his eyes.

They told her all she needed to know: this wasn't about the menu anymore. It was about Rory and the argument. Luca had gone against her just to piss her off and get the upper hand.

"Soup?" Erin cocked her head, rage sizzling through her veins. She couldn't remember ever being this angry before — angry and betrayed. If she couldn't leave the bloody restaurant for a few hours without finding out everything had been changed, how was she supposed to run the place? How was she supposed to trust her staff? "We don't sell fucking *soup*, Luca! What are you doing?"

"Maybe we *should* sell soup." Luca shrugged, crossing his arms in a way Erin suspected had only been done to accentuate his biceps. His chef's uniform was covered in red stains: tomatoes or beans. If he wasn't careful, it would be blood. "It's going down a storm."

Erin scoffed, biting down on her tongue to keep from exploding. "You're unbelievable. I *told* you not to change my menu without my permission. Who do you think you are? You had *no* right —"

"You've been making the same four dishes for over a year, Erin!" Luca exclaimed, extending his hands dramatically. "It's fucking boring!"

"*Soup* is fucking boring!" she retorted. "If you're not happy with the dishes, you talk to me. You don't go behind my back and do whatever you want! And if you're going to do that, make it a better bloody soup than carrot and coriander."

"Talk to you? You mean like *you* talked to *me* about the waffle man living in your flat?"

Erin was one snarky reply away from steam curling out of her ears. "I *knew* that's what this was about. You're hitting back at me for the other day. You're a *child*, Luca."

Luca batted his hand and shook his head. "Whatever."

"No, *not* 'whatever.' I warned you about this. I *told* you —"

"What are you going to do, Erin? Are you going to fire me? You'd be ruining yourself if you did. It's the busiest time of the year. You don't have time to search for a new line chef, and none of the fools in there have it in them." He motioned with his head in the direction of the kitchen. Cruel amusement danced in his eyes, and it left nausea swirling in Erin's gut. She hated him. She hated everything about him: that cocky smirk, the way he belittled and undermined her hard work, the way he looked down his nose at her because she kept her menu simple and familiar instead of serving a spoonful of fish eggs for a few hundred quid like his other restaurants did.

She hated that he was right. For once, Luca was right. She needed him, at least until the Christmas buzz died down. She didn't have time to find someone new and train them up when they were already so rushed off their feet. His absence would wreak havoc in the kitchen.

Acid seared her tongue, but she kept her voice steady as she said: "You're not irreplaceable, Luca. I don't care if it's busy. You're on your final warning. If you go behind my back again, you *will* be fired."

"We'll see." He made to leave then, but Erin wasn't done.

"We're over," she said. "I'm breaking up with you."

Luca spun back around on his heel, surprise darkening his features for just a moment. "Because of him? Do you like your men penniless now?"

"No." Nostrils flaring, Erin offered a saccharine smile. "Because of you. I *don't* date arrogant, entitled arseholes."

"You used to." He left before she could reply, the door swinging closed behind him.

Erin sunk into her chair, her bones still humming with ire. She was ashamed to have ever let the man into her bed, let alone her kitchen, and now she would have to pay the price until she could find a replacement line chef.

For the first time since she'd bought Spuds 'n' Puds, the restaurant didn't feel like hers. It was tainted, unsafe, a place that drained her and left her heart heavy. She had to go home. She'd deal with the fallout tomorrow, but tonight, she had to go home.

Seven

Lying to his family left a chunk of heavy lead in Rory's gut. But what was the alternative? Telling his mum and sister that, up until a week ago, he'd been living in his food truck?

His mum's eyes had lit up when she'd walked into Erin's apartment. Louise, his sister, had gushed about his fancy pillows and the view of the canal, which reflected a silhouetted barge and its rippling, golden lights tonight. Even his best friend, Jay, who, after his own experience with homelessness, wasn't materialistic in the slightest, had complimented the shiny kitchen tops and the paint job of the walls and doors.

And Rory had gone along with it. It was too late to back out.

They waited for him at the dining table now while he hovered over a pot of rice in the kitchen. His chicken steamed in the frying pan, crispy-skinned and doused in lemon juice. He relished in getting to cook tonight. Though he made all sorts of tasty desserts every day, it had been a while since he'd had free rein in a kitchen with a main course. At least he could take credit for something in the flat, now. At least he'd done something to earn the praise.

As he was setting out the rice and chicken on the plate, the front door swung open. Rory frowned, wringing his greasy hands on a tea towel as Erin stepped in. Her face was pale, nose pink from the cold, hair falling just slightly out of its usual neat bun. Her glassy eyes sharpened at the sight of three strangers at her dining table, and she straightened quickly, keys rattling in her hands. Rory hadn't expected her back so soon. He'd reminded her of the dinner yesterday, and Erin had been adamant on staying away to leave Rory his privacy. Not that Rory would have minded, though he wasn't sure how to explain away her presence in 'his' apartment now.

"Oh, bugger. Sorry. I forgot you had the..." she motioned to Mum, Louise, and Jay absently, "thing. Guests. Sorry. Let me get changed and I'll be out of your hair."

"It's alright. I made enough for five in case you were hungry later on. Join us."

"Yes. Join us," Louise agreed, tearing apart a piece of bread caked in peanut butter. Pregnancy hormones had awoken a savage hunger in her, and she'd begged Rory for something to tide her over until the food was ready. "And while you're at it, tell us who you are."

"Oh..." Erin shot him a worried glance, tugging her lip between her teeth.

"She's my roommate," Rory explained quickly.

"Your roommate?" Louise repeated, disbelief fringing her words.

"I thought this was a one-bedroom." Mum glanced between them, flummoxed.

Of course she'd caught them out. He shouldn't have given them the bloody tour earlier.

"Well..." Here it was then. Rory would have to tell them that he was sleeping on Erin's couch like the charity case he was. And worse, he'd have to tell them that he'd lied to them all night. "The thing is..."

"Oh my God." Delight twinkled in Louise's green eyes as they darted to Erin. "You're his girlfriend, aren't you?"

Rory's heart stilled in his chest, his breath squeezed out of his lungs. He tried to stutter out his denial; couldn't.

And then Erin broke into a toothy, meek grin, her cheeks flushing with colour. "Alright, you caught us."

What?

Rory almost choked on his own tongue, his spatula suspended in midair. Behind him, his creamy tarragon sauce was bubbling, and yet he couldn't move to take it off the stove.

"I knew it!" Louise exclaimed.

Jay wiggled his eyebrows, hiding his smirk behind his clasped hands. The closest to Rory, he whispered: "Nice one, mate."

It was Mum who he was most worried about, though. Rory had never introduced her to any of his partners, both because the relationships had lasted so briefly that he'd never needed to and because Mum was no stranger to heartbreak, and that made her protective of her children. It had taken her two years to warm up to Louise's wife, Melissa, and even now, with their first child on the way, she still grilled her from time to time at family get-togethers.

She pursed her lips together, her piercing eyes scrutinising Erin from head to toe. "You didn't tell me you were seeing anyone, Rory."

Erin sidled over into the kitchen. The open-plan apartment didn't afford them the luxury of a private conversation, so he could only cast her a look of distress. "Well... it's early days."

He turned his back to his family, the space between his shoulders blazing against Mum's stare as he salvaged his sauce. "You didn't have to do that," Rory whispered as Erin's warmth tingled at his side.

"It's fine." She sighed, ironing out the cricks in her neck before turning her attention to the food. "Sorry again. I completely forgot."

"It's your apartment." He shrugged nonchalantly before poking his spoon into the tarragon sauce and tasting it. It was... fine. He'd made better. Something was missing, but he couldn't figure out what. Erin would probably know. "Here, taste this."

Without thinking, he pushed the spoon to her lips, cupping his hand beneath to make sure it didn't spill on her no doubt expensive tiling and clothes. Her eyes closed in surprise, her tongue poking out to clear the sauce from her lips before opening her mouth expectantly.

Sweat began to gather in Rory's hairline, at the nape of his neck, under his arms, along his palms, as she tasted the sauce. The way her lashes fluttered on high cheekbones, the way her tongue slipped out a second time, the way she hummed just slightly...

It left Rory tingling. Left heat coiling in his gut. He hadn't realised how intimate it would have been. Maybe he should have. He'd been fighting thoughts of Erin since accidentally glimpsing her naked body last week. There was no denying she was beautiful, intimidatingly so, and... well, the rest of her hadn't been bad, either, though he'd pretended not to have seen. His body couldn't forget though. If he'd had time, he would have taken a cold shower. Thank God she hadn't seemed to notice.

"Did you use white wine?" she asked finally.

"No..."

She tutted. "Should have used white wine. It's good, though. Maybe needs a little bit more salt and fresh garnish."

Rory couldn't have afforded the white wine. The salt and garnish, he could do, though. He plated up, drizzling the creamy sauce on top of the chicken and fetching an extra plate for Erin. "Cheers. Take a seat."

"Hang on. I'm going to need something stronger than lemonade for this." Erin rooted through her cupboards to pull out… white wine, of course. Rory had forgotten all about refreshments, to be honest, and with his sister pregnant and Jay T-total, he wouldn't have bothered anyway, so he'd left out a bottle of lemonade on the side and hoped it would be enough. Which it had been, until Erin had turned up. "Wine, Mrs. Peterson?"

"Aye, go on then, if you're offering," Mum said. "None of that 'missus' business though, thank you. Haven't been a missus for many years. You can call me Wendy."

Erin blew the wiry baby hairs from her eyes as she poured two glasses, her chest heaving with a sigh. Guilt roiled through Rory. His mum was a lot to handle, and Erin hadn't signed up for this. But when she finished pouring and stared unseeingly into drinks, glassy-eyed and deflated, he remembered how desolate she'd looked upon entering.

Something else was wrong. Work, probably. Maybe the boyfriend. Maybe something Rory didn't know about, because he didn't know her well at all, and had to keep reminding himself of that.

"You alright?" he murmured lowly in her ear.

With a sharp intake of breath, Erin snapped back to attention, picking up the wine glasses with a mechanical enthusiasm. "Splendid. Here you go, Wendy. Cheers."

She sat down at the table beside Rory's empty chair, introducing herself to Louise and Jay properly as Rory served up the tarragon chicken. Rory watched her warily. Her smile didn't meet her eyes, her laughter forced. Something wasn't right, and Rory itched to know what.

He took his seat beside her, their knees brushing beneath the table. The contact left him fidgety, his stomach tugging as though demanding more. He distracted himself by slicing into his chicken.

"So, go on then. Tell us everything," Louise urged, tucking straight into her food as though she'd never been fed. "How did you meet? How long have you been together? Why has my brother been keeping you a secret?"

Rory rolled his eyes. There went a peaceful family meal. Maybe he should have just told them the truth. "*Louise.*"

"Oh, I'm sorry. Has your sister not earned a right to know about your relationships?"

Erin cleared her throat, dabbing the down-turned corners of her mouth with a napkin. "Well, like Rory said, it's early days." She placed her hand atop his, laid out on his placemat. "We actually met at work. He's renting out the space next to my restaurant for his food truck."

"Oh, you own a restaurant?" Jay cocked his head, an impressed smirk dancing across his lips beneath a golden smattering of stubble. "Rory's punching well above his weight, then."

Mum sniffed, nibbling on a spoonful of rice. "It's the other way around. No one's too good for my Rory."

Rory squirmed in his chair. He wanted to shrivel up and die, but all he could do was focus on his plate and hope nobody noticed the red splotches searing his cheeks.

"Mum," Louise scolded playfully. "You're embarrassing Rory in front of his new girlfriend."

"What about you, Jay?" Erin diverted the attention to the other end of the table skillfully. "What do you do?"

"Me? I'm a plumber. Nothing special."

"Well, we all need good plumbing, don't we? I wouldn't even know where to start."

Erin's words surprised Rory. He'd expected a swift remark to shut the conversation down, a sign that she didn't really care about a working-class man and his standard job — but she was right. Everybody needed plumbers, just like everybody had needed joiners when Rory had been in the market. And yet they'd still looked down their nose at him when he'd tread into their fancy houses wearing dusty work boots.

He was glad Erin wasn't one of them. Maybe he shouldn't have underestimated her.

"Truth be told, I've only just got back on my feet." Jay's knife scraped against ceramic. Rory winced on behalf of Erin's fancy, patterned plates. "Lost my last job and then my wife kicked me out of the house this time last year, but Rory helped me set up my own business and recommended me to his clients. Business has been booming since."

"That's great." Rory blazed beneath Erin's gaze, and he glanced at her, perhaps lingering longer than he should when he caught something glistening in her eyes. Something like awe. "Rory's a good man. You must be ever so proud, Wendy."

"Oh, I am." Wendy braced her elbows on the table. "What about your family? Will we get to meet them?"

Uncomfortably, Rory scratched at his jaw. His mum couldn't have known, but he still wanted to interject, somehow. How could he without speaking over Erin? He only knew that she was no longer in contact with Thomas, her dad, and her mum had died years before Rory had ever stepped foot on the farm.

"I'm afraid not." Erin tore her hand away from Rory's, and it left him cold, hollow. He wanted her touch back. He was colder without it. "I'm not really in contact with my dad, and my mum passed away when I was younger."

Mum's stern features softened with sympathy. "Sorry to hear that. Family's so important. It must be awful not to have any around."

Beside Rory, Erin shifted in her seat, and his heart stammered and writhed as though her pain was his. Without thinking, he searched for her hand beneath the table. Instead, he found her thigh, his thumb landing on the knobbly hinge of her knee. He squeezed, just once: to tell her he was sorry, to tell her he understood, to tell her he was there.

He changed the subject quickly. "When's the sprog due again, Louise?"

"Not long now. January, with any luck. I'll be fuming if she comes before Christmas, though. Haven't bought her any presents, have I?"

It was something only Louise would worry about. Rory shook her head, relaxing as the conversation eased into general chit-chat: Wendy's bingo nights, Louise's new nursery, Jay's terrible dating experiences. Erin laughed when required, charming enough that even Wendy laid off the interrogations, but Rory still felt something... off. She was tense, quiet, and guzzled her first glass of wine before quickly going for a second.

He wished he knew why. He wished he could see into her brain and find the reason those cogs were turning behind her eyes so furiously so that he could find a way to stop them. But he could only sit and pretend and let the flat fill with his family's tales and warmth.

Without Erin's usual personality, there was still an empty, draughty cavern in the corner. Rory tried — and failed — not to notice.

Erin wilted like a flower in winter almost as soon as Rory's guests left. They'd been lovely, and

Erin had genuinely enjoyed getting to know them, but after the fight she'd had with Luca, the break-up, all she really wanted was ice cream and a marathon of Richard Curtis movies. It was why she had completely forgotten that tonight was the night she was supposed to be avoiding the flat.

"I'm so sorry," she said now, yanking her hair out of its tight bobble and massaging her sore scalp. "I didn't mean to impose like that. And making you lie to them about us…"

"Don't be silly. You did me a massive favour. *I'm* sorry that you had to put up with them." Rory went straight to the pile of dirty plates and loaded them into the dishwasher. Erin made herself useful by collecting the empty glasses from the dining table.

"No, they were lovely." She lowered to prop a wine glass on the shelf at the same time that Rory placed a dessert plate in the same spot, leaving them to clatter raucously. Erin winced against the sound. A headache had been building behind her temples for hours now, made worse by all the wine she'd drunk. "Sorry."

"You sit down. I'll sort this out."

For once, she didn't argue, collapsing onto the couch and kicking her heels halfway across the room. One of them landed on a branch of Rory's dead, lopsided Christmas tree, an extra decoration among the tinsel and baubles. She had to admit that she was warming to it. The golden lights left the evenings cosy, warm, twinkling, and Erin found herself staring at them when she should have been catching up on emails or watching the TV.

"So are you going to tell me what's wrong?" Rory's voice echoed from the open-plan kitchen before another clattering of plates rent through the peace. And then the dishwasher door slammed and the rinse began, and there was no hiding from him. His tall, broad frame eclipsed the tree and the TV, his lips pursed with concern.

Erin kept her eyes trained on the closed curtains, a slither of light from the streetlamps outside slipping in through the gap. "What do you mean?"

He sat down beside her so that that wasn't an option, either. She had to look at him. Had to face him. His arm stretched across the back of the couch, hand inches away from her neck, and she thought of how it had felt to have those same fingers biting into her thigh softly, reassuringly, when Wendy had asked Erin about her family. She could have chalked it up to the fact that they were pretending to be dating — only nobody else had been able to see Rory's one small act of reassurance beneath the table. It had been meant only for her.

It had left her skin sparking, her stomach knotting, chest reeling. It shouldn't have. Not now, not after tonight, but it had.

"You're... out of sorts," he mumbled, crossing one leg while the other dangled off the couch. "You have been since the minute you walked through the door. Bad day?"

That was an understatement. She wished Rory hadn't asked, because the question summoned a stone in her throat, one she'd been trying to swallow down all night. She didn't know why her chest ached so much. It wasn't really for Luca. It was for herself; for not seeing it sooner. For sleeping with a man who was trying to take control of her restaurant, who didn't respect her authority at all. It was sly, what he'd done. Underhand. It was a betrayal; one she was only now letting herself feel properly.

"Hey," Rory said softly as tears began to gather in Erin's eyes. His hand found hers, the pad of his thumb tracing slow circles across her knuckles. "Erin, c'mon. You're worrying me now."

God, she thought she'd shaken off this sort of weakness years ago. Bosses weren't supposed to cry, were they? They were supposed to be ruthless, untouchable. And yet here Erin was, exhausted and heavy-hearted and stung.

"Sorry." She sniffed, pressing the heels of her palms to her eyes. She counted to five. Took a deep breath. She was better than this. She wouldn't cry over Luca. Her hands came away dry. "Sorry, I'm alright. Really."

"You're not."

"I am!" she snapped harshly, and then instantly regretted it. But if it fazed Rory, he didn't show it. Didn't even blink. "Sorry."

"Stop apologising. Talk to me. Please. Or at

least tell me it's not something I've done."

"Of course it's not you. You'd know about it if it were you."

He chuckled at that.

She tugged a loose piece of skin from her nails so that she wouldn't have to look at him. "I broke up with Luca today."

"Oh…"

Erin had expected more than just an "oh." She didn't know what — a "how awful" or maybe even a "good" after the way Luca had treated Rory — but not just "oh." The word hung in the air between them, an icy draught, and Erin pulled the blanket draped across the back of the couch onto her knees to protect herself from it.

"I'm not heartbroken or anything," she explained. "It's just… well, he's a bit of a prick really, isn't he?"

Rory raised his hands as though in surrender. "You said it, not me. What happened? Why now?"

"I told you he kept changing my recipes?"

"Yep, I do recall."

"Well, I was out of the restaurant for bank meetings and whatnot today, and I come back to find a new sign up with a soup of the day. Chuffing *soup*, Rory. Carrot and coriander. I don't even *like* soup. Soup has never been on the menu. Never. Who walks around the Christmas markets and thinks: 'y'know what I fancy? Soup'?"

The corners of Rory's mouth twitched with

suppressed amusement. "No one sane, certainly. Not with all the waffle trucks and cheese stalls about."

"Exactly!"

"Well, for what it's worth, I think you did the right thing. If he can't respect you as his boss, he probably doesn't respect you at all — and the minimum you deserve is respect, Erin."

The words, so genuine, so delicate, eased her twisting stomach just slightly. That Rory understood; that he saw it from her perspective… "You don't think I'm overreacting? It's just soup, at the end of the day."

"It's not just soup." He found her hand again; squeezed; left it in her lap with hers, intertwined. "It's going behind your back. It's trying to control something that's not his to control. Some men… they think they know better. It's arrogance. If you can't trust him with your menu, Erin, what can you trust him with?"

He was right. It wasn't just soup. Luca hadn't been able to see that. He'd tried to manipulate her, tried to make Erin feel silly for reacting the way she had. But she'd deserved to react that way.

She deserved better.

"You're right. Thank you."

Rory nodded, his dark eyes focused on their locked hands. Erin didn't want to pull away; not yet. It had been eons since she'd felt this comfortable with another person. She didn't even enjoy holding hands usually. She didn't feel the need for physical contact — not with anyone, not even with Luca unless they were having sex.

But this, here... She was leaning into Rory, and Rory was propping her up, and it was what she'd needed all day. Maybe a lot longer. So she let him keep holding onto her.

"Fancy watching some telly?" she asked.

The ice cream and rom-coms could wait.

Eight

Erin hadn't realised just how badly she'd missed her best friend until she was standing in front of her, haloed by the golden lights of the markets, the elegant architecture of the town hall rising up behind her.

Rani had spent the autumn with her family in Pakistan, and the majority of the year she spent travelling for work, so Erin rarely got to see her these days. That she'd come back just before Christmas was a blessing. After the last few weeks, Erin was in dire need of a conversation with someone other than her co-workers and Rory. Not that there was anything wrong with Rory. He was just... a man. And, if she was being honest with herself, maybe she needed to talk to someone *about* him. Just for a second opinion. Not because she was thinking of him night and day or anything. She definitely *didn't* keep catching herself remembering the touch of his fingers feathering across her knee in the shower or in bed when she should have been sleeping.

The problem was that wherever she was, whatever she did, he was usually there, too: in the apartment, outside her work, on their lunch breaks. It was difficult to stop thinking of someone who was always around.

Rani extended her arms as soon as she caught sight of Erin approaching, and Erin fell into them with a relieved laugh, squeezing her best friend tightly. "It's been so long."

"*Too* long," Rani agreed. "We have so much to catch up on, and I have so much shopping to do. We have to talk while we walk."

Erin didn't have a say. Rani tugged her along by the hand, knitting them back into the crowds of Thursday-night shoppers. Truth be told, Erin was just about sick of the markets by now. She passed through them almost every day, and the smell of fried onions and beer lingered permanently outside the restaurant. Still, she linked arms with Rani and pretended to be interested in the stalls for her benefit, even if she had seen them a hundred times. Rani told her that she was searching for a bracelet for her mother's birthday, and, knowing Mrs. Ahmad, who Erin had met plenty of times now, only the best would do.

In other words, it was going to be a long night. Luckily, Erin, for once, had had time to change after work and had rooted out her comfortable boots and jeans for the occasion. It had been a long time since she'd dressed casually, normally, instead of restricting herself to blazers and pencil skirts and tights that always ended up laddered. She felt more herself than she had done in months. And she didn't have to shout at anyone for burning her potatoes tonight — though she did have to suppress her temper when a child stood on her toes while rushing over to the cake stall.

"So… Tell me about you." Rani wiggled her dark brows, running her index finger across a turquoise-stone necklace that was definitely too tacky for Rani's mum. "Are you still seeing the dishy Italian man from your restaurant?"

"*Ugh*, no." Erin kicked around an abandoned marshmallow and then regretted it when it stuck to the sole of her shoes. "That's over and done with now."

Rani gasped. "*What*? Why?"

"He ended up being awful. I want to fire him, too, but I can't do without a line chef at the busiest time of year."

"But… Italian." Rani pouted. She'd been a bigger fan of Luca than even Erin had, despite the fact they'd never met.

"But… wanker," Erin retorted with a shrug, and then searched for a way to change the subject. She found it in an elegant rose gold ring. "What about this?"

"She hates rose gold. Says it makes her itch." With a roll of her eyes, Rani inched down to the next stall, which sold personalised toys and Christmas baubles. Erin narrowed her eyes at the first one she came to. 'Rory' had been etched into the painted wood, as though she needed a bloody reminder of the man still living in her flat.

And yet her stomach fluttered, just like it

did most nights. She'd found herself excited to go home to him recently. They'd cook dinner together or order takeout, and just... chat. Like it was normal. Like he belonged there. The flat had been silent and echoey and lifeless before, and now it was filled with his gravelly voice and deep laughter and awful Christmas playlists.

And then she felt guilty, because she shouldn't have been thinking about going home to pyjamas and a home-cooked meal and Rory. She was here, with her best friend, who she hadn't seen in months. Why couldn't she stop thinking of him, just for a few hours?

"Hell*o*?"

She at least had Rani to snap her out of it — which she did, quite literally, by clicking her fingers in Erin's face impatiently.

"Earth to Erin. Do you copy?"

Erin sucked in a breath, scolding herself as she burrowed further into her scarf. "Sorry. Daydreaming. It's been a long day."

"Hmm, yeah, a long day," Rani muttered, sounding unconvinced. "I know that look. It's the one you had in every bloody marketing lecture for three years."

Heat crawled up Erin's face. She had spent a lot of time at uni worshipping her marketing lecturer, Kath — but to be fair, her rich, dulcet voice would have served more purpose on the radio than in a lecture hall, with an Irish lilt to it that Erin could still hear. It wasn't Erin's fault she had a weakness for Gaelic brogues.

"Don't know what you mean," she said anyway, walking swiftly past a stall of strudels before she ended up giving into temptation. "Do you fancy a drink?"

"Do *you* fancy *someone*?"

"No!"

"Is that why you broke up with Luca?" Rani pressed. "Oh my God. Who is it? Are they fit? Where did you meet them? Have you had sex yet? Are they rich?"

"Stop!" Erin squeezed her eyes closed as though her lids could protect her from the barrage of questions. "I'm not seeing anyone, and I definitely *don't* fancy anyone. I'm single and don't want to mingle."

"Liar." Rani pinched Erin's arm through her coat, eliciting an "*Ow!*" from Erin. "Tell me. It can be my Christmas present."

Erin slapped Rani's hand away, scowling. "You don't celebrate Christmas."

"That's no reason to not give me a gift! I'm your best friend! I deserve this!"

Erin pursed her lips in frustration, ignoring the sidelong glares thrown her way by the stall owner. They were blocking the queue and clearly not going to buy any of the cheeses laid out on the table. Erin didn't care; she glowered back for good measure before wandering away. Luckily, the final cabin on the strip sold mulled wine. "If we're doing this, I'm getting a drink."

"Fine. I'll have a tea."

"S'pose I'm paying then," she grumbled before getting in line. Rani lingered by one of the round, high tables, placing her bags on the stool opposite her own. Apparently, she'd done plenty of shopping before meeting up with Erin.

Erin returned with two mugs, placing them on the table before shifting Rani's shopping bags to take a seat. A faux candle flickered in a mason jar between them, supported by tinsel and garland. The amber light danced across Rani's features, leaving the glint in her eye to appear all the more wicked.

"Go on then," she urged, warming her bare hands on her mug. "Out with it."

Warily, Erin blew on her hot wine before taking a sip. It was too sweet, too citrusy, but it warmed her belly and left spices lingering on her tongue. "Fine. There was this guy who I *maybe* had a *teensy*," she pinched her finger and thumb together to show just *how* teensy, "crush on when I was younger. And maybe he has recently made a reappearance and is now sleeping on my couch."

"*What?*" Rani's tea sprayed across Erin's face without warning. Stiffening, Erin blinked and wiped the spatters away with her gloved hand.

"Cheers. I needed a shower, as it happens."

"He's sleeping on your *couch*? *Why*? Why not in your *bed*?"

"We're just friends."

"*Pfft.* I might have believed it if you weren't

blushing."

Erin swallowed and pressed a hand to her face as though it might chase away the evidence. She did feel hot. "I'm not blushing. Anyway —"

"Erin?" A voice interrupted her, trembling and hoarse. She frowned, finding a tall, greying man hovering by their table. His eyes were pale, icy blue, lips thin, chin cleft. Familiar, and not just because the features were similar to her own.

She knew him, though it was disconcerting to see him here, now. Her chest felt as though it was being pummelled by iron fists.

It had been years. She'd never expected to see him again.

"Dad."

He was just… standing there. Outside a Selfridges in the middle of Manchester, wrapped in a scarf and a sleek, navy coat, brown paper bags clutched in both hands. And on either side of him, a child. A boy and a girl.

"I… Wow. You…" Dad stuttered, lips bobbing open and closed like he was impersonating the goldfish they'd won at a fair once when Erin was younger. "I can't believe it's you."

Erin pushed away her mulled wine. The bitter, fruity smell was making her nauseous, and she wasn't confident that the few sips she'd already taken weren't going to make a reappearance. Acid churned through her gut, rising up her oesophagus. She wanted to disappear. She wanted him to stop looking at her. She wanted to go back to the reality of sixty seconds ago, where her biggest problem had been the roommate she was attracted to.

She'd always pictured Dad wasting away somewhere after she'd left Yorkshire. Maybe he'd get by with a minimum wage job, most of which he'd throw away again on his poker games. Maybe he'd get help, go to therapy, join a support group.

But this... this image of him here, now, cleanly shaven and doused in a decent-smelling cologne... it didn't compute. It didn't match up. And who were the kids? His? Had he... God, had he had a second go at the whole dad thing and done it better this time?

The thought plunged a knife through Erin's gut.

"How are you?" Dad asked, as though she was a friend from work he'd bumped into rather than a daughter he'd failed and hadn't spoken to for over a decade.

"Fine." It was all Erin could bring herself to say. She glanced at Rani desperately, but Rani only looked confused. She had no idea who he was, and why should she? Erin barely did, either. "Thanks."

"Good. Good." Dad nodded, glancing at both of the children in turn. "This, er... These are my two little'uns. Chloe and Joel. Kids, this is Erin. Your sister."

The children's faces scrunched with confusion. Clearly, they'd known as much about Erin as she had about them.

A brother and sister. She had a brother and sister. She *was* a sister.

Something glinted in the corner of Erin's vision. She glanced down, finding a silver wedding band catching the light on Dad's finger. He'd remarried, too. He'd moved on. Erin still ached from her childhood, but Dad had moved on. If she were a better person, she might have been happy, but as it was, she could taste only bitterness, feel only white-hot anger.

"I'm Rani," Rani introduced, her melodic voice severing the tension. She extended her hand, shaking Dad's awkwardly as the bag rustled in his hands. "I'm a friend of Erin's."

"Pleasure. I'm Erin's Dad, Thomas. Kids, why don't you go and find Mum a minute, eh? She's over there by the scarves, see." He pointed to a middle-aged, dark-haired woman perusing a rack of knitted scarves and fur hats, oblivious. She was pretty. Not like Mum was, but Dad had struck gold — for a second time.

At least he hadn't messed it up yet with them.

The kids wandered away, and Erin was glad. What was she supposed to say to them? How was she supposed to smile and be friendly when they were just finding out about each other now?

Rani pushed off her own stool, too. "I'll leave you to it a minute, shall I?"

"No… Rani —"

Erin's pleas made no difference. Rani ambled

in the other direction with her cup of tea, casting Erin an apologetic glance as she did.

And then it was just the two of them.

Dad was wise enough not to try and sit down. They both remained frozen, Erin on the stool, Dad standing with his bags, his wrinkled face wan. And then he placed the shopping down, scratching his jaw. "I can't believe how grown-up you are. I mean… " His eyes flitted from the crown of her head to her toes. "Wow."

"Yeah." Erin fidgeted on her stool. "Tends to happen after a decade or so, doesn't it? Ageing, I mean."

"Erin…"

She scraped a hand through her hair, loose instead of tied in a tight knot for once. "I'm not sure what to say to you. I'm not sure what you want me to say."

Dad's brows drew together, jagged lines etched into his forehead. "It didn't feel right to just walk past you like you were a stranger."

But I am, Erin wanted to say. *So are you.*

"Well…" It was her attempt at wrapping the conversation up. She should have known it wasn't as easy as wrapping a gift. Sellotape wouldn't hold them together. There were no neat little bows to make this better.

And Dad asking, "How have you been?" only made her feel worse. Because real fathers would already know the answer to that. What was she supposed to say? Was he asking how she'd been since the age of sixteen, when she'd moved out? How she'd been recently? How she'd been at university, graduation, building her business, going through a first heartbreak, a second, a third? How she'd been when she'd struggled to move her sofa into her apartment alone? How she'd been when she'd fallen down the stairs of her apartment building and had her leg in a cast for twelve weeks?

He'd missed it all. She couldn't summarise a casual answer to what was usually a casual question. He didn't deserve to know. "Fine. Good. Great, actually."

He nodded solemnly, as though she'd just informed him of a family bereavement. "Good."

"Look —"

"Could I maybe give you my number? We could sit down sometime. Catch up. I'd, er... I'd like to know more about you, Erin. I'd like to be a part of your life again. I've been trying to contact you for a few years, actually, but I couldn't find you. I'm not exactly a whizz at all this Google and FaceTweet malarkey."

A sharp pang jolted through Erin. She didn't know if she was glad or angry that Dad had been trying to find her. There were some things that couldn't be fixed. Maybe he'd have been better off sticking to his new family, his new kids. She glanced back at them now, her eyes glossy and stinging. She didn't know if it was the cold or something else.

All three of them were looking at her: her

two siblings and Dad's wife. For just a moment, she saw her mother instead and wondered what she'd say. She'd been stubborn like Erin. Dad was always in the doghouse with her for something: not pulling his weight around the farm, getting snarky with her when they bickered, getting too drunk at the pub with his mates and succumbing to an awful hangover the next day.

But she'd always forgiven him. Always kissed him at the end of the day and told him she loved him. Would she have done that now? Would she have wanted Erin to let him back in, or move on?

She had an entire family she hadn't known about. If she agreed, it might change everything.

"Maybe," she said finally, pulling out a business card as he jotted down a number on a wine-stained napkin. She wouldn't give him her personal number; just the restaurant's. That way, she could avoid him if she had to.

He inspected the card, surprise flickering across his features. "You work here?"

"I own it." Erin's words came out sharper than she'd intended.

"Bloody hell, Erin. That's fantastic. Good on you."

"Yeah." She snatched his number and shoved it haphazardly in her pocket, not yet deciding whether she'd throw it in the bin later on, or perhaps rip it up and burn it.

"No, really. The kids are obsessed with those

Yorkshire pudding wraps you do." His cheeks lined with a hesitant smile, his waterline glistening with what Erin hoped weren't tears. "God, your mum'd be ever so proud. I'm glad she taught you all her best recipes before…"

Erin winced. She didn't want to hear about Mum. Not now. She didn't want to remember the time they'd all been happy, a family, because then she'd have to remember the parts after. She'd have to remember losing it all.

"Your, er, kids are waiting for you," Erin said finally.

Dad's eyes flitted to his family beyond Erin's shoulder. "Right. Yeah. I'll be in touch, then."

"Okay."

He shifted uncomfortably. "I'm really glad I found you, Erin."

Erin nodded blankly, at a loss. She watched his back as he finally returned to his family, an immediate grin brightening his features. Erin saw the cracks in it, though. She looked away when his eyes fell to her a final time, blinking the haze from her eyes and searching for Rani.

She was already approaching, equipped with another small bag now. Erin hoped that meant the shopping trip would end early. She wasn't in the mood. She just wanted to go home and cocoon herself in her duvet and make the memories go away. She just wanted to be alone.

"Are you alright?" Sympathy softened Rani's heart-shaped face.

Erin wasn't, but she'd gotten good at pretending otherwise. "Fine. Did you find something for your mum?"

"Erin…"

But Erin didn't want to talk about it, so she didn't. Instead, she followed Rani around more stalls, the dizzyingly bright lights burning her stinging eyes and her stomach coiling into a tight, painful lump of coal.

She was fine. She was fine. She was fine.

Maybe if she repeated it to herself enough times, it would be true.

∞∞∞∞

Rory was exhausted. It had been a long week of waffle-making and flat-hunting, and he was no closer to finding anything affordable even remotely near the city. To blow off some steam, he'd met up with Jay after work, and he hoped Erin wouldn't be asleep by the time he got back. Only because he didn't want to disturb her, of course.

Or maybe he'd been looking forward to watching a bit of reality TV on the couch with her before she went to bed. Maybe he missed her warmth when she wasn't around, and maybe he liked to know how her day had been. Maybe he even liked to listen to her rant about complaining customers and how Luca had tried to take a jab at her that day — he'd apparently retired to small things that just about kept him employed, like not crisping up the Yorkshire puddings enough or sprinkling an extra helping of oregano on the roast beef.

They'd settled into co-existing well, and this flat... it sometimes felt like Rory's own personal sanctuary. Everything was okay as long as he was here, as long as Erin was pottering around, cleaning up or cooking dinner or humming soft notes of old songs in the shower. As long as he could smell the earthy roast of her coffee blend or the floral notes of her perfume.

Maybe he was a little bit fucked, actually, but he wasn't ready to admit that yet.

As it happened, Erin wasn't asleep. She was in the kitchen, swathed in steam from four different pans and the open oven. Her hair was tied up messily, her flushed face coated with a light sheen of sweat. Rory checked his watch just to make sure he had the right time, but it still said ten p.m. Around two hours later than their usual dinnertime.

As he stepped in, closing the door behind him, herbs and spices pricked his nostrils. They reminded him of the farm, their home-cooked Sunday roasts. "Er... Isn't it a bit late for..." he checked the pans of onion-littered gravy on the stove and then the still-sizzling baking tray, where lines of crispy Yorkshire puddings sat, "a roast dinner?"

"Are you hungry?"

"No..." He'd grabbed food with Jay only an

hour ago, but at the sharp glance thrown his way, he amended, "Yes."

"Good." She went back to stirring the gravy, her movements not nearly as smooth, natural, as they usually were. She could have made this with her eyes closed, and yet she was jerking about, flustered, flitting between pots and pans and mashing the potato as though it was a dragon and she the slayer.

He frowned, taking a seat at the breakfast bar. "Is everything alright?"

"Fan-dabby-dozy," she mumbled, scraping her escaping hair back before opening the oven door again. It released another wave of mouth-watering aromas: roasted vegetables, garlic chicken, leeks. Erin stuck her hand in to take out one of the trays and — "*Ow! Fuckfuckfuckfuck!*"

"Oh, Jesus." Panic drew him up, the metal legs of the stool screeching against the tiles as he rushed to Erin. She clutched her hand to her chest, trying to shake away the pain. Her face had crumpled with it. Rory took over, pulling her to the sink and trying to pry her hands apart. "Let me see."

She didn't, still hugging her injury tightly to her chest.

"Erin. Please. Let me see."

Reluctantly, she relaxed against him. Rory eyed the angry red welt on the side of her hand for only a moment before forcing it under the tap. It wasn't serious, but it would sting like it was. Rory had burned himself with the frying oil more than enough times to know that.

"Why on earth aren't you wearing oven mitts, you daft sod?"

"I..." Erin flinched against the running water, her fingers trembling. "I don't know. I forgot."

She forgot. As though she wasn't a professional, experienced chef with her own restaurant and a melee of qualifications. It sounded like utter bollocks to Rory. Something was wrong.

He lifted his gaze from her hand, searching her features. Her lips were pressed into a thin line, eyes burdened by dark circles, makeup worn off in patches. A grim unease settled in his stomach, just as it had the night she'd broken up with Luca. She was sad. It felt like she was always sad, and Rory wanted so badly to fix whatever it was. That's what he did. He fixed things. He'd been a joiner, and when he'd quit that, he'd searched for other ways to help.

But he never seemed to be able to help Erin. He never seemed to be able to chase away her problems. He hated it. He hated it more that she wouldn't just come out and tell him. She'd given him shelter, a place to sleep, and she never treated him like an unwanted guest because of it, but she never let him repay her. She never let him in.

He'd just have to pick the locks and wheedle through an entrance of his own.

After a few more minutes of soothing the burn, Rory set her hand free and turned off the tap and then, when he began to smell burning, the oven. "Do you have anything for it? Sudocrem, maybe?"

"It's not that bad."

Rory clenched his jaw. *Stubborn bloody woman.* "That's not what I asked."

A sigh, and then: "In the top cupboard next to the fridge."

He followed her directions, rooting through a shelf of medicines and plasters. He respected her privacy enough not to read the boxes, satisfied when he found a grey tub of antiseptic healing cream and a few cotton pads.

"Sit down."

To his surprise, Erin did, looking anywhere but at him as he joined her back on the stools. She held her hand out, giving him permission, and he dabbed the cream onto the burn as delicately as his clumsy fingers could manage. It was already blistering, but with any luck, the cream would help.

"Tell me what's going on with you," he demanded finally, gently. "Why were you making a roast at ten p.m.?"

Erin's throat bobbed, and he was certain that from the corner of his eye, her chin wobbled, too. It left his heart swooping down into his stomach.

"I was stress-cooking."

"Stress-cooking." Rory frowned, tearing his attention from Erin's hand to slip the lid back onto the cream. He suppressed a smirk, his eyes meeting hers. "Is that like stress-eating?"

"Yeah. It usually calms me down."

Usually. Clearly it hadn't tonight. "And what did you need calming down from? What happened? Something with your friend? The one you were meeting tonight?"

Erin shook her head. "No. I... I shouldn't talk about it with you."

His curiosity only prickled stronger with those words. *With you.* As though he had something to do with it. "Well, you're going to. 'Cos I want to sit down and eat these Yorkshire puds."

Nose wrinkling, she slumped in her stool. "You don't have to eat them."

But Rory was already dishing out whatever wasn't charred onto two plates, dousing it with gravy. "Have to now. They'll be soggy in the morning."

He slid one plate over to her and kept the other for himself, pulling out the cutlery before returning to his seat. Their knees brushed; closer, somehow, than they had been a moment ago.

"Go on then," he urged, risking a forkful of the massacred mashed potato. He usually liked it with a few lumps, but he doubted he'd find any here. "Talk to me."

Erin's fork drifted across her plate without purpose, her face absent. Wherever she was, it wasn't here, with him. He resisted the urge to bring her back.

"I saw my dad tonight. He was just... there. After thirteen years. With two kids."

Rory reached out, his hands curling around hers. She looked at them as though they belonged to someone else; as though nobody had ever touched her before. "God. I'm so sorry. That must have been…"

"Shit," she answered for him.

"Yeah, shit," he agreed. "Did you talk to him?"

"A little bit. He wants to sit down for coffee." Her words dripped with bitterness, tears falling onto her cheeks. Rory's thumb twitched with the need to wipe them away, but he didn't. He couldn't. It wasn't his place. He had no idea how she must have felt, and that she was showing him even a glimpse said enough.

"Are you going to?"

A shrug. "I haven't had a family for thirteen years. I didn't even know he remarried or had more kids. Apparently, he's been searching for me, but…"

"But it doesn't change the pain he put you through," he finished for her.

"No. I can't just sit down in a cafe with him and pretend it's okay."

"You don't have to. Not if you don't want to. But aren't there things you want to say to him?" Rory sidled closer, and he wondered if he'd imagined the way Erin seemed to lean toward him. "Don't see this as his chance to make amends, Erin. See it as your chance to get a little bit of closure. To tell him what he put you through."

Erin shrank in on herself, pinching the bridge of her nose, her eyes welded shut. Rory knew what it meant. Exhaustion, dragging at her. She already wore her pyjamas, as though clothes had been too much to stomach, too heavy, when she'd gotten home.

"What can I do?" Rory questioned, his voice cracking with desperation. "How can I help?"

She shook her head as though she didn't know the answer. Rory pushed away his plate, sighing as he glanced around. The kitchen was a mess, but the piled baking trays and pots weren't nearly as daunting as the way he felt; the clueless-ness, the hopelessness.

He stood up and began piling it all away, salvaging what he could into a stack of Tupper-ware from the cupboard. They had enough York-shire puddings to get them through an apocalypse. Maybe he could find a place to donate them tomor-row.

Shuffling distracted him. He glanced over his shoulder as he began to load the dishwasher, finding that Erin was padding over to the couch. She collapsed into the cushions, curling the blan-ket around herself and turning on the TV. "We have some episodes of *I'm a Celebrity* to catch up on. Fancy watching some famous people eating os-trich testicles?"

Rory's lips twitched with the ghost of a smile. It was as close to an invitation as he'd get, and he seized it with both hands. "There's no better way to spend a Friday night."

Ant and Dec appeared on the screen a moment later. Rory piled away the rest of the dishes and turned on the dishwasher before kicking off his boots and plonking down onto the opposite side of the couch. He was expecting that to be the end of it — it was how they usually spent their evenings — but Erin shuffled closer and offered out her blanket. He understood. She was seeking comfort. Seeking *him.*

Heart thundering in his chest, Rory covered his legs with the blanket. His fingertips dared to dance along her arm, her shoulder, brushing away the stray hairs matted to her sweat-dampened neck. She blinked, keeping her eyes trained on the TV, but he was certain that he felt her shudder.

When she leaned back into his chest, Rory's world stopped. Her warmth pressed against him, her spine digging into his stomach, the hinges of their hips locking into place together. It was all he could think about, and he remained stone-still, afraid that the smallest of movements would send her away; would break whatever dream he'd fallen into. The TV blared, and he didn't hear it. The night wore on, and he didn't feel it. He only felt her breaths, rising and falling against him; her gentle laughs; the hitches in her throat.

They fell asleep that way, and only woke when morning crept through the curtains like an uninvited guest.

Nine

A knock on the door of Erin's office broke her concentration — and she was grateful for it. Numbers and spreadsheets and bills always kept her busy, but they weren't what she wanted to focus on today. She'd had other ideas recently, especially after helping Rory deliver food to the homeless several times a week. It was the least she could do, and she still wanted to help more.

"Come in," she called, putting down her pen and lifting her gaze to the door.

They did, slowly. If Erin had known who her visitor was, she wouldn't have been grateful at all.

Her heart somersaulted into her throat at the sight of her father in the threshold, two take-away coffee cups in his hands and a navy scarf knotted around his neck. When she hadn't heard from him over the weekend, she'd assumed that would be the end of it; that they'd go back to pretending the other didn't exist.

But here he was. Served her right for giving him her bloody business card.

"I haven't seen you for thirteen years and now it's twice in one week," she remarked coldly without deigning to stand up or offer him a seat.

"Lucky me."

"I kept picking up the phone to call you this weekend," Dad admitted, daring to step into the office. The door swung shut behind him. "I didn't really know what to say, and I didn't think you'd answer."

He was right; she wouldn't have. After the initial shock had worn off on Friday night, it had made way for anger: the same anger that had been simmering in Erin's gut for years. Yet she couldn't find the strength to summon it now; to tell him to get out, leave her alone. She tried, but the words snaked around the lump in her throat and then refused to go any higher.

When Erin remained silent, he extended one of the cups. "Hot chocolate?"

Erin hadn't had hot chocolate in years. She fueled herself on caffeine, and probably wouldn't have gotten through the day without a daily minimum of five cups. Still, she took the offer and placed it down on the desk. Dad took it as his cue to sit, too, glancing around with... awe? She supposed Spuds 'n' Puds *was* a far cry from the empty farmhouse they used to live in.

"This place is amazing, Erin. I can't believe how wonderful you've become. Well, you were always wonderful, of course. I just mean... your own office. Isn't that something?" His throat bobbed, his grey eyes locking onto hers. The emotions swimming there — pride, joy, admiration — didn't belong to him. He hadn't earned the right to them.

Erin had built her business, her life, without him, and none of it was his to be proud of. *She* wasn't his to be proud of.

"Thank you," was all she said, crossing her legs uncomfortably.

"How long have you had it?"

"Four or five years, now."

"I always thought you'd go down the agriculture route. You always said it's what you wanted to study."

Erin choked on a scoff. She'd wanted to study agriculture to keep the farm running, just as Dad had before her, and Granddad before him. But that was when they'd had a farm to run. That was when Erin had something to inherit. That was before they'd lost everything. "Things changed."

Dad nodded with grave understanding, his finger trembling faintly against the lid of his cup. "Look, Erin —"

"Why are you here?" she blurted at the same time, no longer able to trap the things she wanted to say. She thought of what Rory had said: that, if anything, this was a chance to get closure. Maybe he'd been right, but sitting in front of Dad, Erin didn't know how closure could ever exist. Not after the things she'd been through. She'd lost both of her parents as a child, not just one — and a hell of a lot more than that, too. Nothing she or he said could change that.

"I told you: I've been searching for you for years."

"Why?"

Dad frowned, slanting his head, and Erin elaborated.

"Clearly you've moved on. You have a new family, new children. What could you possibly gain from this now?"

"It's not about gaining anything, love."

Erin flinched against the pet name and tried not to think of all the other times he'd used it.

Goodnight, love.

Have a good day, love.

Your mum's not very well, love.

We've lost the farm, love.

"The life I have now isn't some sort of replacement for what I lost before," Dad continued. "Chloe and Joel aren't a replacement for you. You're my daughter, and I know I failed you. I know you hate me. But I love you, Erin. That doesn't go away, ever. And I want to try to make things right. It won't be easy. I never expected it to be. But... God, I've missed being your dad. There's not a day I haven't wondered about you. It makes me sick to think of what your mother would say if she were here now to see what a mess I've made."

Erin's sinuses prickled with the promise of tears. She tapped a silent beat onto the side of her cup, trying to school her features into the same mask she used when she was handling a difficult customer or wanted to keel over from period cramps but had to make it through the day. But it wasn't the same. Those things, she could separate herself from. She could compartmentalise, tell herself that it was fine, that it would pass, that she was the one in control of the situation. This, here, now, wasn't something she could push aside or take a few paracetamols for. It was a gaping wound that had gushed with blood and then been staunched and then had gushed again, over and over, for years. It was the shadow hanging around her neck and it was the reason she always spent her Christmases and birthdays alone. It was a pain that never eased. It was the reason she was here, rushed off her feet every day, focused on work so that she wouldn't have room for anything else.

Tears fell, hot and sticky on her cheeks. She patted them down in an attempt to salvage her makeup from streaks.

"Chloe and Joel are dying to get to know you better. Chloe's always wanted a big sister." Dad smiled softly, uncertainly. The love brimming in his words was difficult to ignore. Erin wondered if he'd ever spoken about her that way.

"I don't know what you want me to say," Erin admitted, and despised the way her voice cracked.

"I don't want you to say anything. I just..." Dad ran a hand along his jaw roughly. "Crikey, you'd think I'd be better prepared for this. I've imagined seeing you again for years and years. I've written a thousand different speeches. Practised them in the mirror and everything."

Erin almost snorted at that. Almost.

"I don't want anything from you, Erin," he continued gently. "I can't expect anything from you, either. I can't take back the ways I let you down. But I can say that I'm a different man now. A better man. A better father, I hope. And I bet you're different, too. Wouldn't it be nice if we could just... get to know each other again for the people we are now?"

Erin chewed on the inside of her cheek. She could feel the tender sting of a mouth ulcer forming there, another sign that she was worn out, rundown.

She tried to separate the man in front of her now from the one she'd grown up around. They were worlds apart in so many ways. This one was calm and collected, dapper. And yet all of those things were skin deep. His eyes were still the same ones that had stared unseeingly when she'd begged him to stop haemorrhaging the farm's money. His rough hands still had a faint, crescent-shaped scar from the time one of the horses had bitten him. He was still him, and she was still her, and nothing in the world could make her forget that.

"I don't know," she said.

"I understand." He bowed his head, his broad shoulders sagging. Erin couldn't stand to see that disappointment. She couldn't stand the unease tearing through her. She couldn't stand that her only choices were to turn her back on him for good or let him in again. If she chose the former, she'd also be turning her back on two siblings she'd never had the chance to know.

How could she go home tonight, to an apartment she usually lived in alone, knowing that she had a family out there? Knowing that she was a sister? It would always haunt her, just like Dad's mistakes did.

"Do they really want to get to know me?" Erin questioned meekly, thinking of the two bewildered children she'd seen at the markets.

Dad nodded, animated now. Desperate, maybe. "Joel begged me to ask if you'd come bowling with us on Thursday night. It's usually just the three of us, you see, while the missus has a pamper night for herself. They always thrash me, too. Think they want a bit more competition. And Chloe... She wanted to ask you about makeup and hair and all that girly stuff. She couldn't believe how pretty you looked. Like a princess, she said."

The corner of Erin's lips lifted with a smirk. She didn't know if he was just saying it to convince her to come, or if they really did want to know her. They'd seemed as mystified as Erin had felt on Friday night, and she couldn't blame them.

"What about your wife?" she asked. "Wouldn't she have something to say about it?"

"Alison's been helping me look for you for years. She was so chuffed I finally found you. She wanted to introduce herself at the markets, but she didn't want to overwhelm you." He rubbed his hands together, though it wasn't cold in the office.

"So she knew about me?"

"Of course. She knows everything about my past. Even the terrible bits. I don't deserve her, really, but... she stuck around, and I couldn't complain."

"You're happy, then." The words pressed on her lungs, her ribs, making her feel brittle. It was selfish, but she wondered why he'd been able to be better for them and not for her. Why Chloe and Joel got to have a dad when she hadn't.

"I am happy," he said. "But there's always going to be something missing. I'm always going to have to live with the awful things I did. I can only try to be better. For the kids, for Alison, for you. For your mum, too. I miss her all the time. I bet you do, too."

"Yeah. I do." Erin missed Mum so much that she ached, especially now, when Dad was both a stranger and the monster she'd blamed for thirteen years. But he was right, and she knew that. He couldn't change the things he'd done. He could only make sure he didn't make the same mistakes again.

Did that make Erin his Guinea pig? His test child before the real thing? Or was that unfair, too? She didn't know. She only knew that being without family had never gotten any easier. She only knew that he was here, now, and she didn't want to regret not trying. It would be hard, and it would take time, but...

She steeled herself with a decisive breath

and asked, "Where should I meet you on Thursday, then?"

∞ ∞ ∞

Rory only had time to trough down a stack of his own pancakes in the truck for lunch. The closer it got to Christmas, the busier the markets were — which wasn't a bad thing. He'd earned more money last week than he had for the rest of the year, and it meant he was one step closer to finding a decent flat.

When Erin's head peeked over the counter without warning, he almost choked. "'Ello," he greeted, words muffled by pancakes and syrup.

"Can I come in?"

He nodded and opened the truck's door, holding it for Erin to sidle past. He still wasn't any more used to her standing in his beaten down truck, her fancy suits incongruous against caramel stains and flour-dusted surfaces. She didn't seem to mind, though, instead taking a seat on a stool he'd had little time to make use of between customers.

She blew out a breath and then motioned to the pancakes. "Have you got any going spare?"

Quietly, he shoved the plate over to her and handed her a fresh set of cutlery and a few napkins. He'd overestimated his hunger and more than had his fill after the first two. When she dug in, her brows knitted together gravely, he wanted to ask what was wrong.

For once, though, Erin didn't make him force it out of her. "My dad just turned up in my office."

Rory grimaced, swiping a damp rag along the still-sizzling stove and then running it across the counters. Though it was difficult, he had to keep his personal feelings towards Thomas aside — for Erin's sake. He couldn't blame the man for the things he'd done when he'd been buried in a haze of addiction. "What did he have to say?"

"Just... stuff." She shrugged and then took to rolling the pancakes up and eating them with her hands instead of using her knife and fork. Rory raised his eyebrows, impressed. She must have been enjoying them. *Or* she was stress-eating, which was at least a step down from stress-cooking. Her hand still bore the red mark from that disaster. "His kids want to get to know me, and I said I'd go bowling with them. I don't know why. I think I've made a huge mistake. Should I just leave this all alone? I mean, I've not needed him for thirteen years. What's another few decades more?"

"I think that's your choice to make." Rory sighed and crouched so that he could meet her eye. "But I also think that you're not the type of person to agree to something you don't want to do."

Her chewing slowed at that, and he smirked. He'd caught her out. Maybe he knew her better than she'd thought.

"It's all just weird," she said. "I'm not even any good with kids. What if they hate me?"

"Just don't shout the way you do in the kitchen and you'll be right as rain. I could come if you wanted. I happen to be quite the pro when it comes to bowling." If ending up with the ball in the side gutter half the time counted as pro.

She snorted at that, glancing down at him for the first time. "You don't have to. I couldn't ask that of you."

"Do you want me to?" He *wanted* her to want him to. He wanted to be with her somewhere that wasn't here or the apartment. He wanted to support her, wanted her to feel as though she wasn't alone. He had a feeling she'd been alone for too long.

Hope and something else, something too hot, too sharp, lanced through him when she smiled. "Yeah. Maybe I do."

With a tut, she reached out her thumb. It settled on the corner of his mouth, her touch as delicate as a feather's, and he could do nothing but remain frozen, stunned. His breath caught in his throat, want stirring in his gut. They were so close. Too close. And she was touching him. Why was she touching him? Did she want to kiss him? He leaned in, his lips puckering slightly —

"You've got a bit of syrup on your mouth."

Ah. They hadn't quite been on the same page, then.

Erin drew her thumb away, and then seemed

to think better of it, smearing the syrup across his lips with a giggle instead. Cheeks burning, Rory's bottom lip tugged down with her nail, and he imagined it was her lips, imagined...

She drew away, and he forced himself to stop imagining. It was causing problems, leaving his jeans tight somewhere other than just the waist. Still, there was syrup on his mouth. He could have searched for a napkin, but he poked out his tongue, swiping across the ghost of her touch. If it was as close to her as he was going to get, he'd savour the sugary taste, savour the flames she'd left.

Erin watched him, her lips parting before she tore her eyes away. Good. He felt as feverishly red as a roasted Carolina Reaper pepper, and he was going to combust if she touched him again.

"This is good, by the way," she admitted. "Really good."

"You don't have to sound so surprised." He rose from his jelly-like hind legs, busying his trembling hands by scraping burnt batter from the stove. "It is my job."

"I never knew you liked baking."

He shrugged. "I s'pose I didn't either. Truth be told, it was you who taught me how to work an oven back at the farm. I was useless before that. Anyway, it was always something I went back to. And as you can tell, I got a wicked sweet tooth." He patted his soft stomach, half-covered by his apron. "My sister said I should think about doing it properly, so I did a short catering course after my joinery apprenticeship, but I didn't really know what to do with it. Busy kitchens weren't for me, and I didn't really do fancy food they serve in ant-sized portions. Just decent, ridiculously unhealthy desserts. Stuff I could afford."

His words elicited a chuckle from Erin. She stood up, placing her syrup-streaked plate down on the counter and dusting down her hands. "Well, it works. Actually, I've been doing a lot of thinking recently. I think Luca was right."

Rory pursed his lips at that. Whatever Luca had said or done, it was highly unlikely he'd been right in any capacity.

"Don't worry," Erin reassured quickly. "I'm not going barmy. I just mean he was right about the menu. It needs some changing up. I've been neglecting the dessert side of things, but... what would you think about teaming up? Puds 'n' Waffles. I expanded the kitchen a few months ago, so there's room for a dessert station, and I've been meaning to start looking for pastry chefs, any-way."

At a loss for words, Rory could only stare, wide-eyed. Was Erin offering him a job... in *her* kitchen?

She winced. "You look surprised."

"I am," he confessed, scratching the back of his neck. "Er..."

"You don't have to give me an answer now. Just... something to think about. Maybe I'm over-stepping. You have your own business, and you probably want to keep it that way. I just thought… this would give you a bit more stability, maybe."

He deflated as quickly as the crème brulée he'd once — and only once — attempted to make. Charity. This was more charity. She felt sorry for him. It wasn't enough that he was sleeping on her couch; she felt she had to give him a job as well. Jesus, she really thought him that desperate.

"You've been generous enough, Erin," he muttered through clenched teeth. "I don't need anything from you."

"I didn't mean it like that." She sighed, crinkling her eyes shut. "I worded that wrong. I'm not doing this out of generosity. I *need* a pastry chef. I'll be advertising the job whether you want it or not. I just thought I'd ask you first, because, honestly, there's no one I trust more. Business has been booming. The markets are usually quiet on this street, but it's been packed all month — because people want your food, Rory."

Rory narrowed his eyes, considering her words. A lot of the customers he served *did* appear already clutching a tin foil-wrapped Yorkshire pudding from the restaurant. People seemed to want them both, not one or the other. And a stable job…

He could sell the van; get a better one to use on weekends or days off. Maybe even one with space for Erin's main courses, too, if she wanted. A landlord would be more likely to accept his application if he was employed by Erin rather than never knowing where his next earnings would come from.

It *would* be a bloody good collaboration. Puds 'n' Waffles.

"You're twisting my arm," he admitted.

"Good. Think about it." She patted him on the shoulder as she passed, stopping to say: "And while you're at it, we're having the staff Christmas party on Saturday. Just a pub down the road. Crescent, it's called. You're welcome to join for a few drinks if you fancy it."

Anticipation prickled beneath his skin at that. Getting drinks with Erin... it might be fun. A different sort of fun to sitting on the couch and watching telly while Rory tried not to notice how his heart never seemed to calm when she was around.

"You're full of tempting offers today, aren't you?"

Erin smiled — a genuine, sparkling, spellbinding smile that made her cheeks swell and her eyes crinkle. "Always."

He wished it wasn't the truth.

Ten

Dad's face lit up like a Christmas tree when he caught Erin and Rory approaching. So did Chloe's, who held his hand, a twinkling tiara perched on her head and a pink feather boa wrapped around her neck. Joel looked a bit more tentative, stabbing the toe of his trainers into the flagstones. Erin felt the same.

She whistled at Chloe's outfit as she reached them. "Wow. Aren't you a bobby-dazzler?"

Chloe rocked on her heels bashfully and then fluttered about her feathers. "I'm a princess."

"You came!" Dad beamed. It made Erin's heart wrench; she wasn't sure if it was in a good way or bad.

"And you brought a friend!" Chloe added with a gap-toothed grin aimed at Rory.

"I did! This is Rory." She glanced warily at Dad, wondering if he'd remember Rory. She was surprised that Rory had even offered to come, given their past at the farm — the one Erin still hadn't properly apologised for. She still didn't know the truth about her mother's jewellery, but after living with Rory for nigh on three weeks, there were no longer any doubts in her mind. He was a good person, not a thief. She could trust him.

Which left the greying man in front of them her only suspect. Dad had paled, his eyes flickering with unease, which only confirmed Erin's suspicions.

"Rory Peterson," Rory introduced, extending a hand. There was no malice on his features, no sign of anything but perfect politeness. Too nice for his own good. Erin wished she shared that trait. "I don't know if you remember me —"

"Of course!" Dad's smile spread thinly over hollow cheekbones: forced. "Crikey, you were just a gangly young lad the last time I saw you. I didn't think you two were still in touch."

"We weren't," Erin explained. "Rory owns the food truck set up next to the restaurant. He's hiring the space."

"Utter Waffle?" They were Joel's first words to Erin, and hopefully not his only ones.

Rory laughed. "That's the one. Have you been?"

Joel nodded eagerly. "It's my favourite."

"If you swing by again soon, I'll give you a special discount. How's that?"

Erin almost rolled her eyes. It wasn't fair that he was so good at... well, being a nice person. Better than she was. The kids — her *siblings*, she had to remind herself — would like him more than they liked her by the end of tonight. Maybe bringing him had been a bad idea after all.

"Shall we go in and do some bowling, then?"

Dad asked, chuckling when the kids cheered. Erin and Rory followed them in. Her palms were clammy, and she regretted not wiping them down on her jeans when Rory's hand found hers and squeezed. She shuffled closer to him, his presence a comfort she wished she didn't need to lean on. But everything felt easier with him here. Everything would be alright as long as they went home together tonight.

Erin hadn't really focused on the bowling part of the night. She'd been more worried about the reuniting-with-her-father-and-meeting-her-siblings-for-the-first-time part. So, when they rented shoes at the front desk, she saw that she should have been far more terrified of the dirty insoles, which still bore the sunken-in shape of their last wearer. It was with deep regret that she passed over her own suede ankle boots to collect afterwards.

They seated themselves on a foamy couch outside of the alley. Wrinkling her nose, Erin slid her feet into the borrowed shoes and knotted the laces firmly. They were too big despite being her usual size. She felt like a clown. More so when they walked onto the glossy floorboards of the alley and she almost slipped from the lack of traction. Rory caught her elbow, pulling her close.

"Steady on, love."

Erin laughed breathlessly, linking her arm through his. "Is it too late to change my mind and go home?"

The fact that the kids were already bouncing up and down on the purple sofas opposite their lane suggested that the answer was yes, and Erin didn't have the heart to run away now. As they approached, Chloe gripped her hand immediately. "Come on. It's our go first!"

Joel sidled up to Rory when he sat down, Dad on the other side of him, wearing a shaky smile. Under the silver ceiling lights, sweat shimmered on his forehead.

"Alright, then. Are you going to show me how to do it?" Erin asked.

Chloe nodded eagerly and pointed to the row of bowling balls. "It has to be pink, otherwise it's unlucky."

"Oh, I see." Obediently, Erin slipped her fingers into the pink bowling ball, trying not to acknowledge how surreal it was to see her silhouetted figure in its polished reflection. Bowling was uncharacteristic enough of her, never mind bonding with a family she hadn't even met until today. "How's this?"

"Perfect!"

Erin placed the ball on the ramp for her. "Go on then. Show us how it's done."

Chloe did, giving the ball a gentle push. It ambled down the alley slowly before colliding with three pins on the right edge. Still, she clapped for her own achievement, proud as punch. "Now you have to get the other ones for me..." she cupped her hands around her mouth and whispered, "so we can beat the smelly boys!"

"I heard that, cheeky!" Dad called, though when Erin glanced over at him, he was back to laughing. Rory was, too, and Erin was all too aware of his gaze burning into her back as she turned around to retrieve another ball. Pink, of course. She wouldn't want to ruin their luck.

She placed the ball on the ramp, but was stopped by Rory before she could push it. "No, no, no. Surely you don't need a kiddie's ramp to win, Erin!"

When she whipped around again, she found a challenge dancing across Rory's dark features. Erin narrowed her eyes, fierce defiance warming her stomach. She might not have bowled since adolescence, but she wasn't one to back down from a challenge.

"What do you think, Chloe?" she asked. "Do I need the ramp?"

"No. You have the lucky pink ball."

That decided it then. Erin nudged away the ramp and kissed the ball for good luck, flexing her fingers in the holes. She was just glad she'd worn her best mom jeans: the ones that made her bum look a little bit rounder than it usually did. Perhaps not a thought she should have been having in front of her dad, but... well, Rory was watching. She swung back and —

The ball slipped from her hands, flying behind Erin. "Oh fuc —" *Nope. Children about.* "*Fudge!*"

The ball rolled pathetically to Rory's feet. A peal of laughter caused her to startle again — from Joel. Dad joined in, and then Chloe and Rory, and Erin had to trap her own hysteria.

"Come here. I'll show you how it's done." Rory rose from his chair with the ball and towered behind her.

"No!" Chloe shouted. "No boys allowed!"

"I'm not a boy. I'm a man," Rory replied. "And I'm giving you a discount on my waffles, re-member?"

That pleased Chloe enough that she sat down beside Dad.

"Alright." Rory's voice was a low, hoarse rumble in her ear as he handed her the ball. Erin stiffened as their fingers brushed, wondering if they were about to have one of those moments in rom-coms that dripped with sexual tension. He would teach her to bowl and their bodies would press together. But then he said: "Is now a good time to confess that I'm absolutely terrible at bowling?"

A mangled guffaw escaped Erin's throat, sur-prising even her. "You're supposed to be helping me!"

"Well, I can at least get it onto the alley. That'll be an improvement." He slapped her fin-gers out of the holes to replace them with his own, leaving only her thumb in the ball. They swung back together, his hot breath pooling in the shell of her ear, and she couldn't breathe, couldn't stop noticing his heat against her back, her backside against his hips, her fingers against his palms and thank God he had control of the ball, otherwise she might have dropped it on his bloody toes.

As it was, he swung forward, them skipping down the alley together to release the ball. Erin nearly slipped again, but he caught her. He was always catching her.

Lo and behold, the ball hurtled into every single pin, leaving them to topple down with a clatter.

"See!" His voice rose with triumph, egged on by the kids' cheers. "I'm a pro."

Erin crossed her arms, her face still on fire from their proximity. "No. It was the lucky pink ball, wasn't it, Chloe?"

"Yeah!" Chloe agreed, sticking out her tongue.

Erin sat down. The scoreboard said it was Joel's turn now. Apparently, he hadn't wanted to team up with anyone. Chloe still ended up choosing his ball, leaving Rory, Erin, and her father together on the couch.

She cleared her throat, tucking her hair behind her ear. She'd gotten lost in the game, in Chloe's silly laughter, in Rory's touch, forgetting that her dad was still here, watching.

"So. Are you two..." Dad trailed off, wiggling his bushy eyebrows. "What do the young people call it now? Seeing each other?"

"Oh, no," Erin replied quickly. "Just friends."

Dad nodded, his expression wistful. "I remember when I was 'just friends' with your mum. I always thought you liked each other growing up, though. Erin used to talk about you non-stop when you went home, Rory."

Erin sunk further into the sofa despite the lingering smell of stale, greasy cheese woven into the cushions. "I don't think so. And trying to embarrass me is an odd way of bonding with your estranged daughter."

He chuckled, though it sounded robotic. Wrong. "Actually, Rory, I owe you a massive apology. The last time we spoke… it wasn't on the best of terms."

Rory shrugged. "It's all in the past, isn't it?"

Dad tugged at the collar of his shirt nervously. "That's kind of you, but I'm very ashamed of the way I was back then. It took me a long time to admit I had a problem, but I don't think I'd have any chance of reconnecting with Erin if I wasn't honest about the things I did. The mistakes I made."

"Mr. Levine —"

He stopped Rory with a firm hand. "Please, let me say this."

Rory pursed his lips. Erin's stomach jittered with anxiety, her fingers clenching in the flimsy material of the cushions. "Dad…"

"I took your mother's jewellery."

The air was sucked from the bowling alley, Erin's breath with it. It was confirmation. What she'd suspected, yet so desperate not to believe, had been true.

Dad twisted in his seat to face Erin. "I'm so bloody sorry, love. Of all the things I've done, that was the worst. You cherished that jewellery. It was all you had left of her, and I threw it away for a bloody game I didn't even win."

There was no warning when the tears spilt across Erin's cheeks this time. Dad clasped her hand. She was too frozen, too close to crumbling, to pull it away.

"And I'm sorry, Rory, for letting you take the fall. I was so ashamed, so disgusted with myself. I didn't want my daughter to see me for who I'd become. But she did, anyway. We lost everything because of me."

"Thank you," Rory said, his eyes trained on Erin. She wished they wouldn't be. She wished he didn't always see her at her worst. She wished she hadn't come at all. Sobs were wracking through her, fighting desperately to get out. Over a decades' worth of devastation, finally coming to the surface. "But you had an addiction, Mr. Levine. I wouldn't hold that against you. What's done is done."

She wished he would be as angry as her. He *deserved* to be angry. Erin had lost him, too, that day. Her dad had taken her mother's memory, and then he'd taken her friend.

"That's very kind of you, Rory. You're a good man." Dad turned back to Erin, squeezing her hand gently. "I'm so sorry, love. I'm so, so sorry."

The sobs fell out of her, echoing through the bowling alley. When Dad pulled her into a hug, she couldn't find it in her to pull away. Instead, she cried: for the child she'd been, for the things she'd lost, for him, who wasn't a bad person, but just one who'd made his mistakes and was trying to atone for them now.

She couldn't hate him anymore. She had nothing left to cling onto. Nothing but him. So she did. She held onto her dad as Rory distracted the kids with an offer of milkshakes, and she let the waves wash over her, and she found the first glimmer of forgiveness at the end of what had been a very dark, very long tunnel.

"So…This has been lovely. Really lovely." Erin's father hovered by her car as she unlocked it, thrusting his hands in his coat pockets. Chloe still clung to Erin's hand as though willing her not to go. Rory could only watch, warmth swirling in his chest. He knew how difficult this had been for her, how nervous Erin had been to meet her siblings — even if she hadn't said it aloud.

Erin smiled softly, tickling Chloe's nose with her feather boa until a stream of giggles escaped her. "It has. Really lovely."

Thomas pressed his lips into a thin smile.

"Thank you for coming. Both of you."

Rory nodded. He was glad that he had; glad that Erin had asked him. It meant he'd gotten his own form of closure, too. He'd been fired and evicted from his flat and lived in a truck, and yet he'd never felt as small, as shameful, as the day Thomas had exiled him from the farm for a theft he hadn't committed. Erin had looked at him that day as though she hadn't known him at all. Now, when her blue eyes drifted to him, that ice had thawed completely, and she seemed to laser straight through his skin and bone to his soul beneath. He didn't know when it had happened, only that he was okay with bearing himself to her. He wanted her to know him, trust him. He wanted to carry on whatever this was. He wanted this, here, now, bowling with the family and laughing and letting that flame flicker steadily between them.

He wouldn't let it go easily.

"Can't you come to our house for Christmas?" Chloe inquired, tilting up her head to Erin. Her hazel eyes were round, innocent: infatuated with her new sister. "Both of you? Mum said to ask."

"Oh..." Erin blinked, taken aback. "Er..."

"Chloe," Thomas scolded, his hands landing on Chloe's shoulders to pull her away slightly. "Sorry, love," he said to Erin. "She's a bit over-eager. We all are. Don't feel you have to."

"It's not that. It's just..." Erin's eyes flickered back to Rory again, and the same feeling that always unfurled when she acknowledged him tightened along his skin. "Well, I've been meaning to talk to you about it first, Rory, but I think I'm going to open the restaurant on Christmas Day."

Rory frowned. Erin hadn't mentioned anything like it, and the idea didn't sit well with him. She'd been drained, exhausted, for weeks. She needed the break, and so would her staff. "Can't you pry yourself away from the place for one day, love? How are you going to convince your staff to work on Christmas?"

"It actually won't be a paid workday," Erin said, scratching her nose with the tip of her finger. He'd noticed her doing that a lot recently: a nervous tic, maybe; a sign of discomfort. She might have been terrifying and authoritative and stern, but Rory saw through it all. "I was going to advertise for volunteers. I want to offer free meals for people who don't have anywhere to go. Everyone should get a Christmas dinner, shouldn't they?"

His pulse ebbed to nothing, awe a flight of birds fluttering away in his stomach. He couldn't tell her how proud he was; couldn't find words at all.

He didn't have to. A grin broke across Thomas' face, his eyes crinkling with admiration. Rory was certain he saw tears glimmering just on the surface. "That's a lovely idea, sweetheart. Tell you what: we'll all volunteer, won't we?"

Chloe nodded enthusiastically. Joel bore the expression of a boy who would much rather stay inside with his new gifts, but Rory ruffled his hair and he smiled all the same.

"Sign me up, too." Rory beamed. "I was supposed to be doing Christmas at my mum's, but I'll see if she fancies it as well."

"You..." Erin seemed at a loss for words as she glanced at each of them in turn. "You really don't have to. I wouldn't expect..."

"Nonsense. What better way to spend Christmas than all of us together, helping people who've struggled like we have?" Thomas squeezed Erin's hand, and they shared a look Rory understood well enough: a thread of nostalgia had tied itself between them, reminding them of the farm. Rory remembered what Erin had said about those last few Christmases there: *I suppose Christmas loses its magic a bit after you've spent a few sitting on the floor of an empty house, eating stale bread and butter.*

He could only hope that she'd found that magic again — with him, with her family, with the restaurant. Thomas hadn't always been a bad father. Before the gambling, he'd always made Rory laugh, had taught him all about the animals and machinery with a patience his own father had never shown.

Erin nodded, glossy-eyed. "Thank you."

"Well," Thomas scrubbed his hands together, his breath visible in the freezing night. Beside him, a bright yellow McDonald's sign glowed. "We'd better be off. It's getting late."

"*Nooooo!*" Chloe pouted.

"You'll see your sister again soon."

"You will." Erin crouched and pulled Chloe into a hug, choking on a few pink, glittery feathers as she did. "Christmas Day, eh?"

Joel was next, a little more reluctant to step into Erin's arms — but he did, giggling when she tickled his ribs. "See you later, trouble."

"Alright, then." Thomas clutched his children's hands once they'd said their goodbyes. He was a different man to the one Rory had met just a few hours ago, his shoulders relaxed, his face smooth of troubled wrinkles, full of colour. "See you soon, love."

"Bye, Dad." Erin's voice was uncharacteristically frail as she gave them all a final wave.

"See you, Rory."

Rory nodded politely. "Bye, everyone."

They wandered off to Thomas's car by the bowling alley, leaving Rory alone with Erin for the first time that evening. He gauged her expression steadily across the roof of the car as she blew out a sharp breath.

"You alright?"

Erin smiled, softening slightly. "I am, yeah. Come on. It's freezing. Let's go home."

Home. Like it wasn't just hers anymore, but his, too. Like he belonged there. He hadn't had a home for a long time, and the thought left him floating as he got into the car. They both slid on their seatbelts and Erin twisted the keys in the ignition, but when Rory went to turn the radio on to fill the heavy silence, the light touch of Erin's cold fingers stopped him.

"Rory..."

"Hmm?" he hummed.

"My dad isn't the only one who owes you an apology. I never said how sorry I was for blaming it all on you. I should have."

Rory sighed. He didn't need an apology anymore. Erin had given him more than he'd ever expected just by letting him back into her life, trusting him, putting a roof over his head and believing in his business enough to offer him a permanent job. He'd hated losing her trust all those years ago, hated being accused of something he hadn't done, but he understood. If he'd ever had to choose between trusting his mum or someone else, family would always win. Especially when Erin's father was all she'd had.

"It's in the past, Erin. I can't blame you for what you thought of me then. As long as you know you can trust me now."

"Of course I do." She dipped her chin, sucking in a breath. "But I need you to know. I need you to know that I'm sorry. You were right in what you said in Starbucks that day. A part of me always knew you weren't the sort of person to steal from me. I just... I didn't want to believe it was him. I didn't want to believe that somebody I loved so much could take something so important from me. But it wasn't fair to you. We were friends, and I ruined it."

"You didn't ruin it. We're here now, aren't we? It worked out alright in the end." He didn't say that what they were now felt like something well beyond friends. Whatever they'd shared at the farm when they were teenagers... it had been a weak prologue, a first spark, and now they were lost somewhere in the middle, falling, burning, and Rory didn't want it to end. It was the most real thing he'd ever felt. It made him feel like a man again, not a child posing as an adult while he found a way to lose everything he owned. In finding Erin after all this time, he'd found himself again, too.

Erin only nibbled on her lip hesitantly, guiltily, and he no longer thought about it before reaching out to hold her hand.

"I forgive you, Erin."

She craned her neck to face him finally, her eyes glittering in the low light and a disobedient strand of hair tangling with her lashes. Their laced fingers weren't enough anymore. Rory needed more. He needed to touch her, needed more than he should. He was greedy. Starved. So completely rapt by the way she looked at him; the way her chest rose and fell when she breathed; the way her top and bottom lips curved to meet at the seam.

He brushed the hair away, tucking it behind her ear. The seam unravelled, her lips parting.

"I've been thinking about your offer," he admitted, his fingertips dancing down the crook of her neck. He could have sworn she shivered.

"Yeah?" Erin barely sounded to be listening, and if it was his doing, he wasn't sure he'd ever be able to stop.

"I'd like to accept." Her gaze sharpened again, and he continued before she could say anything. "But I have a concern about us working together."

"What concern?" Her voice was breathy, light.

Rory tilted his head, his heart trying to break free from his ribs. This was it. He could either swallow down his feelings or let them spill out into the car now. Either way, there was something to lose.

But he couldn't keep pretending that he wasn't completely ensnared by her. He couldn't keep pretending as though he didn't want to kiss her and never stop. He'd seen her stony and snappy, just trying to make it through the day, and he'd seen her devastated and unguarded, burnt out and just plain burnt. He'd seen her laughing at the TV with chocolate melting on her fingers. He'd seen her embarrassed. And he loved every version, every piece of her. He wanted more. He wanted all of it.

They weren't just friends. They had never been just friends, and whatever he was risking now, whatever he was throwing away... it was worth it to find out if she felt the same.

"Well..." He licked his lips; cleared his

throat. Erin frowned. "My concern is that I want to kiss you, and I'm not sure if that's appropriate if you're going to be my new boss."

"As your new boss," Erin whispered, "I decide what's appropriate."

She drew into him before he could prepare himself, her fingers knotting in his hair — thank God he hadn't had time for a haircut recently — and his collar, her lips roving across his. The chocolate milkshake he'd brought back for her earlier was sweet on her tongue, her perfume heady and dizzying, and God, he was *kissing* her. He was kissing *Erin*. He couldn't stop. He leaned closer, breathless, his hand snaking to the nape of her neck, where he could feel her hot skin and fine hair against his rough palms.

His tongue lingered, begging for entrance, and she granted it, unbuckling her seatbelt so that she could get closer. Rory had never been so aware of his own body before: he felt Erin in every part of it, from his curling toes to the prickling crown of his head. And at the heart of it, a meteor burning through his stomach, lower, leaving him to plunge through space and past planets, never quite falling into their orbit because she'd already pulled him into hers.

Until she drew away, rosy-cheeked and gulping. "So... Do you want the job?"

Rory laughed. He wanted more than just the job. He wanted everything — and tonight, he had it.

"Yes," he murmured, placing a final kiss on the bumpy bridge of Erin's nose. "Yes, I want the job."

Eleven

Nerves jittered in Erin's stomach as she stepped into The Crescent, a charming, rustic little pub just around the corner from Spuds 'n' Puds — soon to be Puds 'n' Waffles. She wasn't sure why she was so uneasy: because she was announcing the news of her collaboration with Rory, perhaps, or because she was walking in with him and people wouldn't have to look too closely to see what was going on. They'd agreed to keep it professional, but... well. They lived together, and now they were seeing each other, and neither of those things really helped their case.

Most of her co-workers — she hated to think of them as 'employees' — already waited for her inside, bleary-eyed and giddy from the mulled wine and the festive songs ringing out of the speakers. She snatched a mug of her own from a tray at the bar and greeted the sea of familiar faces, drifting slowly away from Rory. To say that she was a stern boss at work, they must have forgiven her for it, because they seemed happy enough to see her now.

Well, most of them.

Luca sat in a booth in the corner, gulping

down a frothy pint and giving her the side-eye. He'd been relatively quiet at work, perhaps because he knew he was hanging onto his job by a thread, but tension still simmered between them whenever they were in the same room. Not the sexual kind it had once been, but a hostility Erin wasn't sure she deserved.

"Speech!" Derek cheered — an annual tradition. Erin sighed, never one to enjoy public speaking, but pressed against his shoulder to step up onto a chair all the same. She had plenty to say today. Better to get it over with.

"Hello, everyone. Thank you for coming."

Another cheer from those who had probably been making good use of the open bar. Erin grinned, catching Rory's eye without really meaning to. He leaned against the bar, smiling, his dark eyes twinkling in the buttery light of the vintage bulbs stringed around the place. She couldn't remember ever being looked at like that before, and whatever she'd been about to say vanished from both her mouth and her mind.

"Er…" She dragged her attention away, back to the rest of her co-workers. No easy feat. "First off, merry Christmas. It's been another successful year at Spuds 'n' Puds, and it wouldn't be possible without you all. Thank you for choosing my little restaurant to work in. I don't say it often enough, but I am grateful. I started off here with a meagre bank loan, an empty building, and a real love of Yorkshire puddings, and to think we've all come so far since…"

Erin swallowed down the lump in her throat, tucking her hair behind her ear before continuing. "Anyway. No crying tonight. It's a party. However, I do have a few announcements to make before we all get shitfaced." Another raucous peal of approval. "First off, I've made the decision to open the restaurant on Christmas Day to offer free dinners to people who need them. Now, I'd never expect anyone to work on Christmas, but if anyone does want to volunteer a bit of time, I'd be eternally grateful. We'll be advertising for any help we can get this weekend and there'll be a sign-up sheet available for anyone who fancies it.

"Second…" Erin took a deep breath, her cheeks feverishly hot from the weight of so many eyes on her. "I'm going for a bit of a rebrand in the New Year. As most of you know, we've had Rory selling desserts in the space next to the restaurant, and it's been a successful venture for both businesses. So, I've offered Rory a permanent space in the kitchen. Our menu has been lacking desserts, and Rory's talent is exactly what we need to rectify that. We'll be renaming the restaurant Puds 'n' Waffles, and —"

A lilting heckle sliced through Erin's speech. *"Bullshit!"*

She frowned, knowing exactly where to find the speaker with such a distinct accent. Luca lounged in his booth, his upper lip curled with derision and his green eyes blazing.

Anger bubbled in Erin. "I beg your pardon, Luca?"

"I said bullshit." Luca rose with a slight stumble and clutched onto the back of a chair for support. "You can't hire *him*." His finger jabbed the air, pointing in the direction of Rory. From Erin's periphery, she saw Rory stiffen at the bar.

"And why not?"

"He's a thief. Has sticky hands. I've seen him."

She narrowed her eyes, thrusting her hands onto her hips. "Seen him do what?"

"He was sniffing around the restaurant around lunchtime today, and then Bethan said the cash register was out of balance when she closed up tonight. Didn't you, Bethan?"

All eyes fell to Bethan, the middle-aged supervisor who'd worked with Erin in the restaurant since the day it opened. Bethan shifted, her eyes darting helplessly. "I was going to talk to you about it later on, but... yes. I'm afraid there's been some money missing from the till."

"Okay." Erin's narrowed eyes shot back to Luca, defensiveness leaving her jaw clenched. "And what makes you think it was Rory, other than the fact that he was in the restaurant?" Which Erin, of course, had already known about. She'd shown him around the place to get a feel for his new environment and then snuck him into the office to have lunch with him.

"Well, he's obviously desperate, for starters.

He's sleeping on your couch, isn't he?"

Murmurs broke out among the crowd. Erin rolled her eyes and stepped down from her chair. "We'll continue this conversation in private, I think. Luca, Rory." She beckoned them into the furthest corner, brushing past low-hanging tinsel and Christmas bunting. They both followed wordlessly, but when she turned around, Rory's cheeks were flushed.

"I haven't touched the cash register once," Rory blurted as soon as they came to a stop.

"I know." She didn't doubt him for a second. "Clearly, there's been some sort of misunderstanding. I'll ask again, Luca. What makes you think it was Rory? Did you see him take the money?"

"No, but who else would it be?" Luca's scathing eyes dragged up and down Rory's figure — brave, considering Rory was half a foot taller than him and twice as broad. "Do you think it's a coincidence? We've never had an issue before. You hire local riff-raff, and then money starts going missing."

Rory rolled his eyes, a muscle dancing in his jaw. It felt like deja vu, somehow. He'd had the exact same reaction when Erin had accused him of stealing her mother's jewellery at the farm. Only now, she knew him. She knew that he would never take something from her; he only ever seemed to give.

Pursing her lips, Erin replied so he wouldn't have to. "You can't accuse somebody of stealing without evidence, Luca. I trust Rory."

"Well, you would," Luca spat, "being as you're probably fucking him, too."

The words dripped slowly through Erin, pooling like ice in her gut. She ground her teeth together, fury coiling through her veins. She couldn't look at Rory; couldn't look at anyone but Luca, daggers shooting from her eyes.

"How dare you?" Her voice came out low; dangerous. Rory's warmth brushed against her back: a reassurance that he was there if she needed him.

"Is it not the truth? Did you not leave me for him?"

The contempt that spewed from Luca... it made Erin sick. She stood firmly between him and Rory, wanting to shield Rory from all so much venom. "I left you because you're a self-absorbed, arrogant wanker."

"Better than him." He nodded to Rory without looking at him, his fists clenching at his sides. "A thieving, poor bastard. He'll spend the rest of his leeching off your success. At least I'm worth something. At least I'm a *man*. Then again, you'll sleep with anybody you can find, won't you?"

"That's enough!" Rory stepped forward, bristling with rage, but Erin pushed him back by the chest quickly, keeping her focus locked on Luca. Rory could do whatever he liked to him after, but it was her turn now.

She'd never hated anybody like this before.

She'd never regretted anything the way she regretted choosing him. "You're fired, Luca."

Luca scoffed bitterly. "Right. Sure."

"I mean it. Go home before I have you thrown out. You can get your shit from the restaurant tomorrow morning."

"You can't fire me! On what grounds? What have I done?"

"If you're such a worthy, wonderful man, you can work that out for yourself, I'm sure." She crossed her arms over her chest. Rory's hand anchored her, kept her stable, and she pressed her back into his chest.

Luca raked his oily hair off his face, speechless. *Finally.*

"I won't ask again, Luca. Get out," Erin commanded.

He jeered. "You'll be fucked without me. I know more than the rest of your cooks put together. I'm the fucking line chef."

"And a shit one at that!" Erin's reply only reached his back; Luca was already marching off to collect his jacket. He sent them both a final glower before leaving, the door rattling on its hinges behind him, and only then could Erin blow out a breath of relief.

But whatever Luca had said and done to her, he'd been a thousand times worse towards Rory. She turned to him, her brows knitting together as she cupped her hand around his stubbled jaw. He was still tense, a string drawn taut, close to snapping. But he softened as he looked down at her, his tongue poking out to wet his lips.

"I'm sorry," Erin said, her voice cracking just slightly. She didn't care if anyone else was watching. Let them watch. It was her restaurant, her choice, and she knew what she was doing. She knew better than she ever had before.

"For what?"

"For him. For putting you in that situation. You shouldn't have had to deal with that."

Rory shrugged and inched closer, ducking his head so that their noses brushed. "You trust me? You know I didn't take the money?"

"Of course I do. Jesus, Rory, I'm not fifteen anymore. I know you. I know you'd never do that. I *trust* you." More than she'd ever trusted anybody. It didn't come easily, but there was nothing about Rory she was afraid of; no shadows lurking behind his light. She trusted him, and she would keep trusting him until he gave her a reason not to, because her heart beat so certainly against his chest and her bones tugged themselves to him as though she was his; as though he was hers.

She knew him, and she trusted him, and it wasn't just her brain and heart that decided it, but her body, too.

Rory shook his head as though in disbelief, his fingers crawling to her chin and resting in the small cleft there.

He dipped closer, his breath fanning across her lips, but the sound of her name being called halted anything that was supposed to come next. Erin drew away, air flooding back into her lungs. She turned around, finding Frankie standing sheepishly a few metres away.

"Yep?"

"Sorry to interrupt…" She glanced between them warily. "Can we maybe talk outside?"

Erin nodded, squeezing Rory's hand once as though to tell him she'd be back before following Frankie out into the brisk night. The streetlights poured amber spotlights over them. A group of drunken men staggered along on the other side of the road, catcalling them on their way. Erin glared. She'd had enough of disrespectful bloody men tonight.

"What's up, Frankie?"

"Rory didn't take the money from the till," she mumbled quietly. Her eyes were glassy — from the cold or something else, Erin didn't know.

Erin watched her curiously. "I know."

"It was me."

A flicker of betrayal speared through Erin. Taken aback, she could only blink as she tried to piece the words together; find a way that they made sense. Frankie was new, but she was kind, sweet, everyone's favourite waitress. Erin had been meaning to offer her a permanent position. "Why?"

Frankie chewed on her bottom lip, rubbing her arms to keep warm. "Am I fired?"

"I don't know," Erin answered honestly. A

few weeks ago, the answer might have been yes. She was still unforgiving then, still trapped as the girl who couldn't trust people, the girl whose father had stolen from her. But then she'd reunited with Dad and she'd found Rory and she'd realised that everybody was struggling to get by. Everybody was driven by their own problems. She couldn't make her decision without knowing Frankie's whole story. "Tell me why and we'll see."

"I'm behind on rent." Frankie's words were thick with the promise of tears. "I'm broke, actually. I know it's wrong. I know it's awful. But I was desperate and the money was just there and... I needed it."

Erin pursed her lips sympathetically. "You should have told me you were struggling."

"I'm so sorry. I really am. It won't happen again, not if you give me another chance."

With a sigh, she stroked Frankie's arm softly. "You're not fired. Just come to me next time you need help. I can put you on more shifts, if you want, and we can talk about a raise. Tell me how I can help and I will."

Surprise left Frankie's eyes wide. "Really? That's it? You're not... angry?"

"No, I'm not angry." Erin brought her in for a hug, thinking of how awful it had been when she'd been broke; how much she wished she'd had someone to look out for her, to try and help. Someone she could rely on. "We've all been there. And if you want a permanent job instead of just a seasonal one, it's yours."

"Thank you, Erin. Thank you so much."

"Of course." Erin smiled, her tension dissipating. Luca was gone. Rory was inside. The restaurant was about to become something so much bigger than it already was, and she was using it for good.

It was all she could hope for. She went back inside with Frankie and tried to enjoy every moment of it.

∞∞∞

Rory couldn't pretend he wasn't glad to be home. Though the Christmas party had significantly improved after Luca's departure and they'd all ended up singing an out-of-tune rendition of 'I Wish It Could Be Christmas Everyday' on the karaoke, Rory was still exhausted.

He could tell Erin was, too, if not also a little bit tipsy. He'd ended up driving them home, and she'd walked up the stairs to her apartment barefoot, complaining of blisters caused by new, glittery shoes. He'd carried her up the last flight.

She collapsed onto the couch as soon as the door swung open, a groan leaving her. Rory smirked, kicking off his own boots before locking up and joining her. She lifted her legs so that he could slip beneath them, running his hands along her stocking-covered shins.

"Are you alright?" He was worried. Angry. The way Luca had spoken to her had been vile, and it had taken everything in him not to throw him out of the pub himself to shut him up. But somehow, Erin had been the one to defend Rory. His heart still fluttered with that knowledge; with the memory of hearing her say that she trusted him, her voice free of any doubt. He hadn't had to explain himself or deny Luca's allegations. She'd just believed him. .

"Tired," Erin mumbled, resting her head on the cushion. Her eyes fluttered shut, and Rory wondered if she'd gone to sleep. He hoped not. He wanted to talk to her. He wanted just a few moments of quiet whispers with her before she went to bed and he slept on the couch. They were taking things slow — or rather, she was, and he wasn't pushing it. He was wary, what with them living together. He didn't want to rush her, smother her, get too attached too quickly.

But their living situation was soon to change either way.

"Erin.".

"Hmm?"

"I..." He blew out a breath, nerves buzzing around his stomach like wasps. Part of him didn't want to say it, yet. He liked it here. He'd found a home here. But he couldn't stay on her couch forever. "I think I've found a flat."

Erin's lids snapped open, her legs tensing beneath his hands. "Oh..."

Oh? He didn't know what that meant. He didn't know if he was just imagining the disappointment dragging her voice to a low, deflated rasp.

"I was wondering if you'd come to the viewing with me tomorrow. I trust your judgement more than I trust mine, to be honest."

A line sunk between her brows. "Where is it?"

"Not far. Salford." Closer to the restaurant than Erin was, anyway. It wasn't his ideal location, but it would do for a year or two. And it meant he'd stay central — both to the restaurant and to Erin. He'd thought it through plenty, probably more than he should. There was a spare room for when Louise's baby was born and a decent kitchen for him and Erin to flit about in — if she wanted.

He hoped she wanted.

"Ah." Erin nodded. "Okay. Nice."

"So will you come?"

"Yeah. Yeah of course I will." She pulled herself up, curling closer to him. He had to stifle a moan of pleasure when her fingers traced spirals along his cheek, into the rough stubble along his jaw and chin. He'd never get used to the way she felt; the way she touched him as though he was delicate, breakable. With her, maybe he was. "Are *you* okay?"

"Me?" He raised an eyebrow. "Yeah, I'm okay. Why wouldn't I be?"

"Luca…" she whispered. "The way he talked

about you."

"He doesn't matter." Rory drew his own patterns along the hard bone of her shin absently. "I had you fighting in my corner, didn't I?"

"Always." The intensity of that word drew his gaze up in surprise. It was murmured like an oath, like she truly meant it. He believed her.

They'd come so far from who they'd been all those years ago. Rory didn't know what he'd done to deserve Erin letting him in like this, letting him see her without the shields and the swords she'd wielded when they'd met again all those weeks ago, but he was glad for them. He wouldn't take the gift lightly, and he'd return the favour with the same raw sincerity that twinkled in her eyes.

"'Spose I need to advertise for a new line chef." Erin sighed, tucking her head into Rory's chest. He breathed carefully, lightly, afraid to disturb her or send her away. But she didn't move, and he curled his arm around her, running his fingers through her hair. The musky, spiced smell of wine and old furniture still clung to her from the pub.

"It can wait 'til tomorrow."

Erin nodded against him in resignation. He looked down to find her dozing off again.

"Come on then." Rory planted a kiss on the top of her head before urging her up. "Bedtime for you."

But Erin didn't move, instead straightening to look at him through a faint, silver haze of exhaustion. "I want you to stay with me tonight."

Rory's breath hitched. He hadn't been expecting it. Not so soon. To be like this with her, be this close, all night... he wouldn't sleep much. Still, he accepted, letting her pull him up by the hand.

They no longer needed to sleep with a wall between them.

Twelve

Erin couldn't find anything wrong with the flat in Salford. In fact, it was about as good as he could have gotten in the city without paying an extortionate amount. The landlord had seemed nice, too, and the lease was twelve months.

She should have been happy for Rory, but as they walked back to the restaurant that evening — they had wanted to avoid the city traffic — she only felt… sad. Hollow. Rory was moving out. Her apartment would be silent and empty and dark again, just as it had been before he'd moved in.

Head bowed, Erin thrust her frostbitten hands in her pockets. It was Baltic, and she'd left her bloody scarf, hat, and gloves in her office. Rory's arm brushed hers with each step. He'd been ecstatic when he'd seen the flat, and rightly so. Why couldn't she be, too?

"Alright. What's up?" he questioned finally, stopping her in her tracks with a light tug of her elbow.

She feigned confusion with a frown, stepping in to let a cyclist past. "What d'you mean?"

"You've not spoken a word since we left the flat. I can hear the cogs whirring in there." He tapped on her forehead lightly. "Did you not like the place?"

"The flat was lovely. Perfect, like you said." Which had only strengthened the blow.

"So why do you look like you've dropped a tenner and picked up a penny?"

She wrinkled her nose, jigging her knees to stay warm. "I don't. I'm fine."

Rory blew out a breath, and it curled between them with the truth Erin couldn't bring herself to say: she'd lost more than a tenner. She'd lost her roommate. "Erin. It drives me mad when you don't talk to me. Please."

She couldn't resist him when he begged. She cared about him too much. She didn't want to push him away because she was being a brooding idiot with attachment issues. Worrying at her lip, she leaned against the shuttered, graffitied window of a derelict vape shop. It rattled with her breaths. "I suppose I'm just sad that you'll be moving out. I liked having you around."

"Oh, right. And I suppose I'm not allowed to use that big metal thing with wheels on to come and see you whenever you want me to?"

She pushed him playfully, her teeth beginning to chatter. "You know what I mean. It's not the same."

The smirk dancing across his lips disappeared, and he laced his fingers through hers. "No, it's not and I'll miss it, too. I'll miss you. Even your snoring, which I can hear through the wall, by the way."

"That's yours echoing through the living room."

He rolled his eyes; pulled her closer still, until she was flush against him. His gloved hand rested at the base of her back, and she had to arch her spine to look up at him. As she did, he peeled off his scarf and coiled it around her neck instead. It smelled like his aftershave and the waffle truck: spicy and sweet, dizzying. She nestled into it, remembering a time when she'd been caught in the rain with Luca. He hadn't offered her his jacket or his umbrella. She'd been peed wet through while he'd strolled through Manchester, warm and dry and dandy. There was no comparison between him and Rory, but it still struck her sometimes how far she'd come. Even when she'd thought she'd been in control of her life, strong enough to be the best version of herself, it had been an illusion.

A broken one now. This was real, and Rory looked out for her, and if the generosity wasn't enough, the proof blazed just as brightly in his eyes.

Something cold distracted her: a fine, damp sprinkling on her nose. She looked up and found powdery snow drifting from the swollen clouds above, more visible against the streetlamps. Rory tilted his chin to the sky, too, a laugh rumbling from his throat.

"Look at that. Snow."

She lowered her gaze. In the north of England, snow in December was a miracle to marvel at, but so was Rory. She watched his lips tilt with a smile, watched his throat bob beneath dark stubble, watched his thick lashes catch the white flakes. And then he caught her staring, and something softened in him, enough to melt the snowfall back to dreary British rain. Her chest eddied with something she wasn't quite ready to put a name to yet: something warm as a November fifth bonfire and colourful as the fireworks that followed.

He pulled her in by the scarf, pressing his lips to hers. His beard brushed against her icy skin, his arms folding her in, keeping her warm, and she couldn't think of any place in the world she'd rather be than on this grimy backstreet in Salford with him.

"I'm so glad I found you again," she whispered when he pulled away.

Rory's answering smile was crooked and toothy and perfect. Snow dusted his hair, his shoulders, sprinkling a wall around them that nobody else could pass through. "Always hoped you would."

Epilogue

Erin had been slightly worried that nobody would show up on Christmas Day. She shouldn't have been. The restaurant was packed, and more visitors flooded in by the minute. Luckily, she'd spend the last few days preparing, and there was no chance of running low on food anytime soon. Erin weaved through the restaurant, chatting to visitors, serving heaped plates of roast dinners, making sure everybody had a cup of tea or coffee. It was chaotic and her soles were already throbbing, but it was exactly what she'd hoped for.

She sidled back into the kitchen to check on her volunteers. Understandably, not all of her employees had wanted to give up their Christmas Day, but she had Derek and Mavis armed to the teeth with spuds, gravy, and Yorkshire puddings, and Rory was taking care of the meat and trimmings, leaving the waffles to Frankie after a brief training from Rory with the batter yesterday.

"'Am running out o'hands, Erin," Derek called, juggling four plates precariously in his arms. "Can you 'elp me bring these out?"

"Yep, on it." Erin rushed to the plates, whipping around on her heel to take them away when her spine collided with something hard. "*Oof!*" She gripped the dishes tighter, only just avoiding a gravy-soaked dress.

Hands clenched around her waist, squeezing tightly. "Sorry, love. My fault."

It had been Erin's actually, for not looking where she was going, but in her stressed state, Rory was clever to take the blame. He'd adapted to her tempers well, it seemed. Despite her haste, she turned to face him, grinning when he placed a soft peck on her sweat-coated forehead. "How's everything out there?"

Erin blew out a breath. "Hectic. Good, though. Everyone seems to be enjoying Puds 'n' Waffles' debut."

They hadn't changed the sign outside yet, but the menus had already been redesigned, one placed proudly on each table. They were set for a grand reopening in the New Year, but Rory was already a part of the restaurant in all the ways that counted, and he'd sign the contracts next week.

"Erin!" A shrill, excited shout pierced through the chaotic din of the kitchen. Erin grinned and turned around, finding Chloe bustling in. She wore an elf costume complete with bells on curly-toed shoes. Joel hadn't gone to such festive extremes, though he did sport a nice bit of tinsel around his neck. Behind them, Erin's dad beamed through a fake white beard, a red Father Christmas hat perched on his head. Alison held his hand, offering a sheepish wave. Erin hadn't had time to properly introduce herself to Dad's wife yet, and her heart thrummed with nerves as she laced her hand through Rory's and dragged him over — for moral support if nothing else.

"You all look amazing!" Erin praised, tugging on Chloe's flaxen plait playfully. "I wasn't sure if you'd still be coming."

"Of course we would," Dad said softly. "Wouldn't miss it, would we? Besides, Alison's been mithering me about meeting you."

"It's good to finally get the chance," Erin replied politely. It wasn't a lie. Alison had kind, round eyes a lot like Rory's, and it was clear just from the way she'd held back that day at the Christmas markets that she didn't want to overwhelm Erin too much. "Thank you so much for coming."

"Thank you for inviting us." Alison's cheeks swelled happily. "Where do you want us?"

"Well, Chloe can help me serve the food, can't you?" Carefully, Erin held out one of her plates, and Chloe took it with two tiny hands obediently.

"Joel can help me," Rory offered. "Do you like pigs in blankets?"

"They're my favourite."

"They won't be when you've wrapped two hundred of them. Come on." Rory led him to his workstation, casting a reassuring smile over his shoulder. Erin watched his back for a moment, wondering how she'd managed to deserve somebody with the spirit of spring sunshine, especially when she'd always been more like winter frost. But he thawed her sharpest, iciest parts, and she just hoped she could offer him something in return. Something as special as he was to her.

She dragged her focus back to Dad and Alison. "Would you mind helping with drinks out front?"

"Sounds grand to me," Dad said, tugging Alison back out of the kitchen.

Erin drew out a long breath before looking down at Chloe, still clutching the plate with the utmost care.

"Right then," she said. "Let's do this, shall we?"

$$\infty \infty \infty$$

Rory's family turned up later on that afternoon: his mum, Louise and her wife, Melissa, and Jay. It was perfect, really. The hubbub had ebbed, the last remaining diners enjoying their meals in the quiet. Rory greeted them joyfully, drawing each one of them in for a hug and pointing them to a seat.

"So glad you all could make it! Have you eaten yet?"

"No. We wanted to wait for you, love," Mum replied, casting a scrutinising eye around the restaurant.

Jay leaned back in his chair, puffing out his cheeks and patting a bloated stomach. "I've just gotten back from my mam's. I'm done for." And then he raised an eyebrow towards the kitchen. "Don't have any dessert going though, do you?"

Rory rolled his eyes, biting back a laugh.

"So this is your girlfriend's place, is it?" Mum sniffed as though she wasn't quite sure how she felt about it.

"Actually, it's our place." Pride swelled in Rory's voice, and he couldn't find a way to quell it. He was too happy. More than happy. Ecstatic. He had a steady job doing what he loved, with someone who believed in him, cared about him, trusted him. "Well, Erin still owns it, but... we're partners now. Puds 'n' Waffles."

"Congratulations, Rory!" Louise praised, punching a light fist into his torso. It was about as affectionate as she'd get. "Now go and get food. The baby is hungry."

"On it." Rolling his eyes, he ambled back into the kitchen, stopping to chat with a few diners as he did. He recognised a few of them from the last few weeks spent offering out meals with Erin.

In the back, Erin was dishing out a hefty pile of mashed potatoes, Chloe standing on a footstool to drizzle on the gravy once she was done. Her family had ended up staying all day, and that was how Rory knew that Thomas was desperate to make things right. Good. It was the least Erin deserved.

He crept up behind her now, snaking his arms around her waist. It tugged a gasp from her, one he quickly stifled with a kiss. Now the kitchen was quieter, he could get away with snogging his boss — he hoped, anyway, because it wasn't stopping him now. "My family are here. Fancy sitting down with us for Christmas dinner?"

Erin's lips curved beneath his. "Sounds perfect to me. What do you think, Chloe? Are you hungry?"

"For waffles," she nodded.

"Well, dinner first, then dessert." Erin laughed and broke free of Rory's embrace to finish up the last few plates. Rory's stomach grumbled against the warm, herby smell of sage and onion stuffing and roasted parsnips. He'd been waiting for his meal all day, and it was making him light-headed now. "Why don't you go and tell your mum and dad to take a seat?"

Chloe skipped out of the kitchen, the bells on her shoes jingling.

Erin turned around, clapping her hands to garner everyone's attention. Most volunteers had gone home hours ago, but a few still remained while the last diners drifted in and out. "Right, everyone. I'm endlessly grateful for all the work you've all put in today. We've done something really special, and I'm proud of us. You've all earned a massive Christmas dinner, so get yourself a plate, sit down, and tuck in."

The kitchen staff all slumped with relief,

and Erin picked up her plates before she was mowed down by hungry volunteers. Rory helped, following her out with three colossal portions. He placed them down in front of Mum, Louise, and Melissa, glad to find that Thomas, Alison, and Joel were all being dragged over by an eager Chloe, too. Erin was armed with a jug of Buck's Fizz and poured everybody a drink — save for Louise, of course, who pouted while she sipped her water and mumbled, "Can't wait to get this baby out of me," as well as Jay.

With everybody ready to dig in, Rory sat down, too, not a minute away from becoming completely ravenous and using his hands. But Erin had other plans. She tapped her wine glass with her fork, remaining standing at Rory's side. Everybody fell silent.

"I just want to say... well," she sucked in a shaky breath, her eyes filling with tears. Rory softened and knotted his fingers with hers reassuringly. "Last Christmas and most of the ones before, I spent my day eating microwave meals and watching TV in my apartment alone. To see that now I'm surrounded by two wonderful families who have taken time out of their own special day to help me here... it's not something I'd ever take for granted. Thank you all so much for coming." Throat bobbing, she lowered her gaze to meet Rory's. A shiver crept along his spine, down to his toes, his heart wrenching with... love. It was love. Of course it was love. Maybe it was too soon, but he knew Erin enough to be certain about what he felt. He knew he'd never felt this way before. He knew that, out of all the people in the world he'd ever passed in the street or fixed up stairs for or served a stack of pancakes to, she was the one who'd been meant for him.

"And thank you especially to Rory, who inspired me to do better." Erin continued. "This is only the beginning for us — Puds 'n' Waffles — and I truly can't wait to see where we go from here. Thank you for agreeing to do this with me."

"Thank you for letting me," he breathed, his fingers crawling up to her elbow. He was glad when she sat down, glad he finally had the chance to kiss her. He kept it brief for the sake of his family; briefer still when Erin pulled away with a gasp.

"Sorry. I forgot to say cheers! Oh, and Merry Christmas!"

"Cheers!" Everyone laughed and clinked their glasses, Chloe spilling orange juice all over the table cloth and Jay guzzling down his coffee in one. Rory glanced around at each of them and felt at home, wreathed in golden fairy lights and sparkling tinsel as he was. They were his family. A strange, not quite conventional family: all of them with their hardships, all of them pushing them aside to be here today with him.

Rory couldn't help it. He clasped Erin's hand again, smiling at her with the love he hoped she felt, too. Maybe he couldn't say it yet, but he could feel it and he could show it, and that was enough.

She beamed up at him, rosy-cheeked, vibrant, and he was certain the image would sear itself into his memory for many Christmases to come.

And then she tore away and snapped, "Tuck in, then! It's getting cold!" before shovelling a heap of stuffing and mash into her mouth, and a chuckle escaped him before he did the same. He was sure that anybody walking by the restaurant that night, past closed up market stalls and shuttered shops, would see it, too, through the garland-decorated window of Puds 'n' Waffles: that unbridled joy, a family brought together over good food and even better company, and at the heart of it all, a man who was completely, irrevocably smitten by the woman who had made it all happen.

It was certainly a Christmas to remember.

About the Author

Rachel Bowdler is a freelance writer, editor, and sometimes photographer from the UK. She spends most of her time away with the faeries. When she is not putting off writing by scrolling through Twitter and binge-watching sitcoms, you can find her walking her dog, painting, and passionately crying about her favorite fictional characters. You can find her on Twitter and Instagram @rach_ bowdler.

Books By This Author

A Haunting At Hartwell Hall

Dance With Me

The Fate Of Us

Saving The Star

The Secret Weapon

Safe And Sound

Handmade With Love

Paint Me Yours

Holding On To Bluebell Lodge

No Love Lost

Partners In Crime

Along For The Ride

The Flower Shop On Prinsengracht

The Divide